Killa Kounty 4

By: Khufu

Lock Down Publications
P.O. Box 944
Stockbridge, GA 30281
www.lockdownpublications.com

Like our page on Facebook: Lock Down Publications
www.facebook.com/lockdownpublications.ldp

Stay Connected with Us!

Text LOCKDOWN to 22828 to stay up-to-date with new releases, sneak peaks, contests and more...
Or CLICK HERE to sign up.

Like our page on Facebook:
Lock Down Publications: Facebook

Join Lock Down Publications/The New Era Reading Group

Visit our website:
www.lockdownpublications.com

Follow us on Instagram:
Lock Down Publications: Instagram

Email Us: We want to hear from you!

Acknowledgements

Life is without meaning, if you don't try to understand or acknowledge the source from which we all come. Thanks to the "Most High" for making me a vehicle for its life force! I am deeply appreciative. To my lil' homie Marcos for holdin' me down when my so-called day one's left me for dead. You the epitome of a real friend. Brittany, you been in my corner for the longest no matter the situation and I love you forever! To my mother for lovin' me unconditionally—it's an honor to be "Patty's son!" Jihad and Supreme, thank you for helping me see narratives in a different light. One love to my nigga P-nut Da Truth, and the Big Homie Ca$h1 LockDown Publications over everythang! And a special shout out to Angelica! You know what it is.

#FortPierce #KillaKounty #TreasureCoast #772 #LDP

Dedication

I dedicate this book to every mother who lost a child to gun violence.

Rest in Power

Stacey ... Tayda ... Tela ... Lanetta ... Lil Poppa

Art is an imitation of life—Plato

Chapter One

A Cold Summer

Khafre looked Machi in his eyes, as he gripped his pistol. Machi viewed the devil in Khafre's eyes, as he trembled in fear knowing this was his last day on earth.

"Khafre!" yelled Crystal in confusion and sheer terror. "What the fuck, you doin'?"

"Returnin' the favor." *Fop! Fop! Fop!* Khafre squeezed off three shots through the suppressor, planting them all in Machi's face.

"Aaahh!" *Fop!* Khafre planted one right above Crystal's right eye, slumping her next to Machi's bed. All in one swift motion, Khafre tucked his banga, slid out of the room and caught the elevator right when it was opening. To his surprise, Tweet was exiting the elevator to go see Crystal and Machi, but she never looked up from her phone. Khafre slid in the elevator with his head low in his hoodie, and headed to the first floor. When the doors opened, he moved through the lobby in a calm state. Once he neared the exit, two cops rushed in, startling Khafre. He reached for his ratchet, ready to bang it out with the pigz, but to his astonishment they rushed right past him and headed straight for the elevator. Khafre kept it pushing and headed to his whip. *Boc! Boc! Boc!* Out of instinct, Khafre got low and snatched his banga out. He ducked behind a 2020 Land Rover trying to pinpoint where the shots were coming from. The windows were lightly tinted, so Khafre could see two figures moving intently between cars, headed straight for him.

"Ummm huh! Got'cha ass na, fuck nigga!" yelled Hezron, letting off two more shots that shattered the Land Rover's driver window. Khafre raised up over the hood of the Rover and let off three shots, hitting Doughboy in the chest and shoulder.

"Aaahh, fuck!" Doughboy cried, dropping to the ground and clutching his chest.

"You a'ight?" Hezron asked, squatting next to Doughboy.

"Fuck! Yeah, I'm good, nigga. You better kill his ass too."

"On my mama, this nigga dies today!" promised Hezron, getting up to make do to his promise. By this time, Khafre had already slid and maneuvered to his car and was now inside. He started the Camaro, alerting Hezron of his whereabouts. As soon as Khafre shifted the car into drive, Hezron appeared in front of the car, and let off two shots. Khafre ducked and punched the gas. The car ran Hezron over and dragged him fifteen feet away from Doughboy. Khafre hopped out of the vehicle and planted two hot ones in Doughboy's temple. He then walked over to Hezron who was barely clinging on to life, and stood over him.

"What dey do, fam?" Khafre asked sardonically with a furtive grin on his face. "It's been a cold summer, ain't it?" *Fop!* Khafre drilled one in the back of Hezron's head, trotted back to his whip and slipped away.

***

After switching cars, Khafre drove to Naples Florida to have a conversation with Hanna and Samantha. Knowing that their father was a racist, Khafre had already made up his mind to have full custody of his sons. Even if it meant killing their mothers. As he spent time with his boys, he was observant and amazed at how beautiful they were. He noticed that Hassan was the calm one and bore a distinctive mole under his right eye, while Husain was more active and had two different colored eyes. One was green, and the other hazel. A single tear fell from Khafre's right eye, as he interacted with his kids and thought of his father. Even though G-Baby made sure he was taken care of from prison, he vowed to never leave his sons under no circumstances.

"What's wrong, daddy?" Hanna asked, surprised to see a sensitive side to Khafre. Khafre wiped his face, and stood to face Hanna and Samantha.

"Listen. I appreciate y'all rockin' wit' me, how y'all did, and I honor both of you, for giving' me two kings. Because of that, we're forever connected. If y'all ever need me for anything, consider that shit done. Na, this gone hurt y'all more than it's gone hurt me, but it is what it is. I'm takin' my sons with me."

"What?" questioned Hanna face tightening with emotion.

"Yeah, what are you talkin' about?" Samantha added.

"Yo father racist, and Ion want my sons nowhere near him. I want my sons to know what it means to be black, and y'all can't give 'em that!" Khafre stated emotionlessly.

"That's bullshit, Khafre, and you know it!" cried Hanna.

"Is it?" Khafre asked with hostility dripping from his voice.

"If you think that you can just waltz in here, and take our kids, you got another thing coming!" Samantha yelled hysterically.

"You've lost your fucking mind!" Hanna added.

"Ssshh! Stop all that yellin' in front of my kids."

"Fuck you, Khafre!" Hanna retorted.

"I see, it ain't no compromising wit' y'all right na. I'ma pull up on y'all at a later date," Khafre stated, walking off to say his goodbyes to his sons. "I'll be back for y'all real soon," promised Khafre, hugging Husain and Hassan.

"Okay, that's enough. We'll walk you out," Samantha interrupted. Khafre stood to leave and headed towards the front door.

"I really need y'all to work with me on this," said Khafre, turning around to face Hanna and Samantha.

"Bye, Khafre!" Samantha said. Khafre looked past the twins as if he'd seen something behind them, prompting them to look behind them.

Fop! Fop!

They never knew what hit'em. Khafre had swiftly drawn the same pistol he'd just used to kill with and planted one in each of their heads. He stepped over them, and went back in the room to retrieve his sons. On the way out, Husain was sound asleep as his head rested on his father's shoulder. Hassan was wide awake. He'd seen the only two women he knew sprawled out over the floor, who to him appeared to be sleep.

"Ma, Ma," Hassan muttered before being carried out of the house.

Chapter Two

Khafre

It was a little after five when Khafre made it back to Atlanta. He didn't want to risk being caught on surveillance in Hartsfield Jackson's Airport with his sons, so he drove the six-hour drive back to Georgia. When Khafre entered the mansion, Quen and his mother were up watching the news in the living room, seated on a massive sectional couch.

"Bae? Wassup, who you got wit'chu?" questioned Quen. Shantel gave Quen a quizzical look as Khafre pushed past them and laid his sons in one of the many rooms in the mansion. When he came back in the living room, he sat between the two women, exhausted from a long bloody day.

"Ladies," Khafre said. He kissed his mother on the cheek, then Quen on the lips, before setting his attention on the news.

"Whose kids you got?" asked Quen. Khafre ignored her as he listened to the reporter describe his killings as "The Hospital Massacre."

Watching his demonstrations make the news was like a euphoric high. It was his aphrodisiac. Clips of the hospital surveillance footage appeared regularly, but for some reason Khafre's face was distorted. Quen and Shantel glanced at each other with a knowing look. Khafre's face may have been distorted, but his distinctive walk was irrepressible. When the news clips were done playing, Khafre sat back on the couch, and noticed both women staring at him.

"Wassup?"

"Bae, that was you?" questioned Quen, already knowing the truth.

"Me what?"

"Really? Don't do that. You know what I'm referring to. The news. Was that you on the news?" Khafre glanced at his mother before replying.

"Yeah. You already knew what time it was," Khafre retorted gallantly.

"I already knew it was you, by that walk, and yo' crazy ass still got on the same clothes," said Quen, shaking her head. Khafre looked his mother in the eye.

"Them niggas tried to take me from you, mama. It's all over with na. I killed everything."

"I'm just glad you okay," proclaimed Shantel, kissing Khafre on the cheek.

"Whose kids you brought in here?" Quen asked.

"Them my sons."

"Yo' sons?" both women said in unison.

"Yeah"

"Never told me you had kids."

"Me neither," Shantel added.

"I just found out tonight. I took 'em from their mothers, they better off wit' me."

"Them kids look like they mixed. Who is the mother?" asked Quen.

"You don't know 'em, but I need to know if you gotta problem helping me raise my sons like they yo' own?" Quen inhaled and exhaled before speaking.

"Of course not, daddy. I'ma love them the same as the one I'm carrying in my stomach." Khafre could feel the sincerity in Quen.

"That's what I love to hear."

"Them my grandbabies, so you know I'ma spoil 'em rotten," asserted Shantel, elated.

"Look, it's been a long day. I'm jaded, I'm finna try to get some sleep." Khafre stood to leave.

"I'll be in there, baby," stated Quen.

"A'ight." Before Khafre entered the hallway, he turned around. "Oh yeah, we moving back to Fort Pierce," he declared and headed to bed.

"I guess," sighed Shantel, shaking her head while turning up the news.

Tonight in Naples Florida, two twin sisters were found at 2310 Tarpon Road in their three-and-a-half million-dollar estate, with gunshot wounds to the head. It appears that the assailant also kidnapped the three-year-old sons of the twins as well. No motive has been established yet, and no suspect at this time. There is a ten-million-dollar reward for any information leading to an arrest.

Shantel and Quen looked at each other as if reading each other's thoughts.

"Khafre!" both women yelled in unison.

Chapter Three

Generational Wealth

After Wolly's people delivered the money for the thousand pounds of loud, Khafre relocated back to Fort Pierce. He'd found a five-bedroom home on Avenue S, down the street from his grandmother Patty's house. The home was secluded away from the others, so inquisitiveness from nosey neighbors was improbable. Even though there were no more threats, Khafre still installed a high-tech security system and nurtured Quen on how to shoot to kill. He was now pulling into the Brownstore on 25th Street to see Wolly. Hopping out of his new 2024 Mercedes Benz EQG, Khafre tucked his .40 in his Bally sweats and swaggered into the store. Wolly glanced at Khafre, then continued to serve a customer. Khafre had grown his dreads to cover the bullet wound so Wolly didn't recognize him.

"Damn, ock, you don't recognize family, when you see 'em?" Khafre asked Wolly. When the customer walked off, Wolly searched Khafre's face for familiarity.

"Khafre?"

"Who else, ock?" Khafre asked, smiling.

"Oh my goodness. Nice to see ya, buddy," Wolly said, coming from around the counter to embrace Khafre. "How long have you been here?" asked Wolly who then locked the door and put the *Closed* sign up.

"I been back for a few weeks."

"Few weeks? My friend, you give me no call? Why?"

"I had to get a lot of shit situated. Nothin' personal. You already know I appreciate everything you did for me."

"No problem, buddy. Anything for G-Baby's son. So, are you back for good?" questioned Wolly, placing his hands on his hips.

"Ain't nothin' like Fort Pierce."

"This place hell hole, buddy."

"It made me, ock," Khafre said. "From the looks of it, it made yo ass too." Wolly smiled.

"I guess you're right, buddy. How was Atlanta?"

"Atlanta was cool."

"Yeah. Did you get the money?"

"Yeah, I got it."

"Good. Should be enough to leave streets alone."

"Shid! A million dollars, ain't shit deez dayz. I want that generational wealth. I got kids na, ock." Wolly took in what Khafre was saying and studied his face.

"I understand. Follow me," exclaimed Wolly, taking Khafre into a room in the back of the store. Once they entered the room, Wolly walked behind what appeared to be a bar. Behind the bar was a huge shelf that contained a variety of liquor. Wolly pulled on a whiskey bottle, and the whole shelf turned sideways, exposing another hidden room.

"Da fuck!" Khafre stated in astonishment. Again, Wolly smiled and waved Khafre in. When Khafre entered the hidden room, one half of the room had walls filled with artillery, and the others were filled with cans of jalapeno that contained dope.

"Wolly, you sneaky motherfucka!" asserted Khafre, grinning.

"Calm down, buddy. Now, as you can see, some of these weapons are primitive, and some are more modern. You can sell the primitive to whoever and keep modern for self."

"Okay, what's with the jalapenos?" Khafre asked, pointing at the cans.

"That, my friend, is heroin," said Wolly, grabbing one of the cans and handing it to Khafre. Khafre grabbed a can opener off the shelf.

"Damn, ock. So, all these years, you been trappin' the whole time?"

"Trapping? No, buddy. Trapping is for small time. Me, I'm boss! There is a big difference, my friend. I sit back, I collect. Eventually you do some. Follow me?"

"I hear you," Khafre said, opening the can, and pulling out a brick.

"Good. Heroin, very pure. Turn one into two. For you, fifty-thousand apiece. I front you five for now. Good?" asked Wolly.

"Fuck yeah, we good!" Khafre replied, elated.

"Good. You want generational wealth? This is how."

Khafre shook Wolly's hand with appreciation in his eyes.

"Thank you. You a real nigga, ock."

***

It was a little after 8:30 p.m. when Khafre left Wolly's. He put the five bricks in the apartment above the Brownstore, and headed home to his kids. Pulling in the turning lane, he took a toke from his blunt, and blew smoke from his nose as he waited for cars to pass by. As the last car passed, Khafre's phone rang. He made a left on 25th and Avenue T, then answered the phone.

"Wassup, mama? Everything okay?" Khafre asked Shantel.

"Yeah, baby. I just finished cleaning my house up. I'm finna roll me up one and watch '*All the Queen's Men*'. Just wanted to check on you, baby."

"Everything Gucci, mama." As soon as Khafre lifted the blunt to his mouth, he saw police lights in his rearview.

"Fuck!"

"What's wrong?" questioned Shantel, sensing that something was happening.

"Nothing, mama," Khafre lied, not wanting her to worry. "I love you, I'ma call you in the morning." *Click*! Khafre hung up the phone, put the blunt out, and put his pistol in the console. He still had the red flag hanging from his pocket, that the Haitian priest gave him in Haiti for protection, so he pulled over. Avenue T was a dark back street, where legendary demonic and horrid acts took form. And on top of that, Taylor's Creek was only twenty feet away. If shit got crazy, Khafre had in mind to go for what he knew, and leave the officer extirpated. The officer stepped out of the police cruiser, approached Khafre's window, and tapped on it with a flashlight. When Khafre let down the window, a cloud of smoke kissed the officer in the face.

"Really?" asked the female officer, aiming the flashlight in Khafre's face. *Damn, this nigga look good*, she thought to herself.

"Can you kindly remove yo mini spotlight from my face, please," Khafre asked nicely. She removed the light from his face. *Damn, this bitch sexy*, thought Khafre.

"It's a beautiful summer night out'chere. What'chu doing pullin' overnice, propitious, prolific, hard workin' taxpayers? As good as you look, you're supposed to be somewhere wit'cha legz to da moon, fuckin' up head boards and shit," Khafre said, looking her in her eyes. Gazing in Khafre's eyes a few brief seconds before responding, she could see pain, murder, and experience behind them.

"I doubt that you pay taxes. And I pulled you because you failed to utilize your turning signal. As an officer of the law, it is my duty to inform you to keep my sex life far away from your thought. I mean, who knows, it's dark back here. I might mistake my gun for a tazer, and air yo ass out back here. Now, license and registration!" the officer stated provocatively, clutching her pistol.

"Damn, boss lady! You'll kill a black man?"

"Air yo' ass out. Now! License and registration!"

"I ain't got 'em, killa."

"Why not?"

"Never had 'em."

"You talk all this tax payer shit, and you don't even own a pair of license?"

"Unfortunately." The officer shook her head.

"Where you headed?"

"Home."

"Where is home?"

"Next street over."

"Next street over, huh? I tell you what. I'ma run your name. If you come back clean, you can go."

"A'ight," Khafre said.

"Name?"

"Khafre Moss."

"Okay, sit tight. Don't make no sudden moves." The officer walked to her cruiser as Khafre watched her in his rearview mirror.

"Damn, that shit thick," he said aloud to himself. Moments later, the officer turned her lights off and exited her vehicle. "I know this bitch ain't run my name that fast," Khafre muttered.

"Mr. Moss, step outta the vehicle."

"For what? I know I came back clean."

"I won't ask you again," she stated, drawing her weapon. Khafre placed his hands out the window, and opened the door. He then stepped out with his hands in the air.

"Calm down, killa," retorted Khafre, trying to pacify the situation.

"Turn around, and put'cha hands on the car." Khafre did as he was told. The officer holstered her weapon, cuffed Khafre and began to search him.

"You got any weapons on you?" she asked, kicking Khafre's legs open, and grabbing a handful of his dick and balls.

"That's on you, to do yo' job, and find out, officer," Khafre replied arrogantly. "And why the fuck, you cut'cha lights off fa?"

"Shut the fuck up and turn around!" Khafre did as he was told. "I ask the questions around this motha fucka! Hear me?"

"Yes, ma'am," said Khafre, grinning jeeringly.

"You wanna tell me, how the fuck you get a 2024 electric Mercedes Benz EQG, and these mothfuckas ain't even out yet?"

"I do a'ight for myself."

"Doing?"

"I own a yacht cleaning bidness."

"I smell bullshit. Stand yo ass right there while I search this mothafucka," demanded the officer, leaning in the driver's seat to search the car with her ass in the air. "What the fuck is this?" asked the officer, spotting Khafre's gun in the console.

"A mothafuckin' Glock .40," Khafre replied, pressing his dick against her thick cotton-soft ass cheeks, and swaying his hips from right to left. The officer pushed her ass back, causing Khafre to stumble. She then turned around and pointed Khafre's own gun at him.

"Bring yo' stupid ass here!" Khafre walked towards the officer who was now seated in the front seat of Khafre's car. When Khafre was inches away from her, she cocked his .40 and placed it under his chin.

"I'ma teach you bout' playin' wit' me," said the female cop, who looked like Ronnie from *The Players Club*. The female cop slipped Khafre's dick from his Bally sweats and began to jack him off.

"Nigga, if you make any type of sound, if you breathe wrong, I'ma blow yo fuckin' head off!" She placed the tip of Khafre's dick in her mouth, twirled her tongue around it, then took Khafre in her mouth whole while looking him in his eyes. Even though Khafre was brimming with excitement about having his dick in a cop's mouth, his face was hard as granite. It took everything in him not to groan or tell her how good of a dick sucker she was. He stared deep into her enchanting brown pupils as she sucked, slurped and moaned. For some reason, sucking Khafre's dick had her pussy the wettest it's ever been, staining her expensive panties. She removed the gun from Khafre's neck, placed it on the floorboard, then made her way inside her tight fitting pants. She took Khafre out of her mouth, let out a short sigh, then placed him back in her mouth. Khafre bit down on his bottom lip, while watching her head bob on his dick to a demented rhythm. She let out a seductive growl as she pressed hard circles on her hood, held it and flicked her clit back and forth.

"Umm—umm," she moaned as her insides clenched and unclenched spasmodically. Feeling an orgasm rising, she placed two fingers inside her, then used her thumb to put pressure on her clit, and creamed all over her fingers. Feeling Khafre grow a few inches in her mouth, she knew he was on the verge of coming. She snatched Khafre out of her mouth, stood up, spun him around and pushed him down into the driver's seat with his hands still cuffed behind his back. Khafre's dick pulsated as she removed her gun belt and lowered her pants. Wasting no time, she eased down on Khafre's dick and rode him reverse cowgirl.

"Ooww—this dick good!"

"Ride that dick, hoe," Khafre encouraged, finally speaking up.

"Sss—shit! Fuck! That's it, give me this dick!" She placed her hands on the ground and began to twerk on Khafre's dick menacingly. It was dark out but her high yellow ass cheeks could be seen bouncing wildly, causing Khafre to let loose in her.

"Damn, this pussy good!" admitted Khafre. She felt the intensity of Khafre's release, and her pussy responded in kind. Sitting up straight, she winded in slow circles and clenched her insides around Khafre until they both were done releasing.

"Damn, officer. I do believe my rights have been invigorated—I mean *violated*." She rose off of Khafre's now extremely wet dick and pulled her pants back up.

"Nigga, shut up. What'chu wanted, pussy or jail?" she retorted, putting her gun belt back on.

"Pussy was fine. Pussy was damn good. Now, can you get deez damn cuffs off me?"

"Wait right here. Give me a second." She walked to her cruiser, sat in it for a few seconds then returned. "Stand up" Khafre stood with his dick still exposed to the night air. She placed his dick back in his sweats, then turned him around.

"What'chu are? A blood or some shit?"

"N'all. I'm too much of a leader to be following another niggas philosophy," Khafre stated arrogantly.

"Then why you got a red flag in yo right pocket?"

"I assure you, this ain't that. I'm on something way deeper." She uncuffed Khafre and turned him around.

"If you say so." She then handed Khafre a ticket and walked back to her cruiser, got in and pulled off.

"This bitch still wrote a nigga a ticket? This shit crazy." Khafre got in his car and examined the ticket. In big

bold letters it read: DICK WAS GOOD! IF YOU WANT
TO DISCUSS DISMISSING THIS TICKET, CALL ME!
772-333-7233. Khafre shook his head, laughed, then pulled
off and headed home.

Chapter Four

Chicken and Waffles

"I want mommy!" Husain yelled brusquely the millionth time for what had seemed to Quen. Khafre heard this as he entered the house and knew that it was Husain, because Hassan didn't act out. Hassan was more reserved and maneuvered as if he'd been here before. Khafre placed his keys on the red marble kitchen countertop and headed to his son's room. When Khafre entered the room, Husain spotted him and was instantly enveloped by silence.

"Hey, dad," greeted Hassan then turned his attention back to "*Coming to America 2.*"

"Wassup?" Khafre replied, then gazed at Husain. "Husain, what the problem is?" Husain shook his head right to left.

"Ain't no problem?" Husain shook his head again before speaking.

"No." Quen watched in silence.

"No? Then what'chu cryin' fa?"

"I not cry."

"You callin' me a liar?" Husain shook his head again

"Come here. Both of y'all." Both boys climbed out of their custom-made car beds and stood in front of Khafre.

"Wipe them tears from yo' face." Before Husain could muster himself to wipe his tears, Hassan wiped them for him. Khafre took a mental note of Hassan's actions.

"Listen, Husain, mommy is gone."

"Nooo!" whined Husain with his head down. Hassan patted his brother on his back, another mental note made by Khafre.

"Hassan, mommy is gone." To his surprise, Hassan looked him in his eyes and nodded.

22

"Okay," replied Hassan.

"While mommy is gone, Quen is goin' to be your step-mom." Husain looked at Quen, his three-year-old mind confused, then turned back around, putting his head down. Khafre put his index finger under Hassan's chin and lifted it.

"You understand me?"

"Yes, dad," Hassan stated. Husain just nodded. Quen sat quietly as tears cascaded down her face. She loved Khafre, but also knew that he was the reason for them never seeing their mothers again.

***

Three weeks later, Khafre had both of his sons in the car with him, as he did pull-ups on every gang leader in the city. His proposal was fifty-thousand a brick, and eight-hundred for state-of-the-art assault rifles. Turning one brick into two, he stood to make five-hundred thousand off of the five bricks Wolly fronted him.

"Y'all hungry?" Khafre asked his sons as he turned the radio down.

"Yes," Hassan stated in a composed manner. Khafre looked in the rearview mirror at Husain.

"Husain, you ain't hungry?" Husain shook his head up and down.

"I'on understand that. You can't talk?"

"Yes."

"Yes, what?"

"I hungry, dad," Husain muttered, playing with his new Rolex that Khafre had purchased.

"A'ight. We goin' to get chicken and waffles. I gotta make one more stop, then we going." Khafre made a right on 14th Street and Avenue D. It was a little after five p.m., a soft summer day, and the atmosphere was *lit*, prompting the streets to be crowded on both sides. 14th Street was

Haitian territory, so it was Zoe's and beautiful Haitian babies everywhere. Spotting who he was looking for, Khafre pulled into the Chinese rice hut.

"Y'all stay in the car. Daddy will be right back."

"K," Hassan replied. Khafre stepped out of his whip in a red Maison Margiela tracksuit, and some *Kyrie Lucky Charms.*

"What up, Nut?" greeted Khafre.

"Wassup, nigga?" responded Nut, hopping off of the trunk of his new Genesis, to embrace Khafre the way gangstas do. Khafre had met Nut during his five-year bid. A riot had popped off between the Pisces and the Blacks, and Nut assisted Khafre when two Pisces had him down bad. After doing time in the hole together, they promised to link up on the outside.

"I'm just koolin', my nigga. I heard you was out'chere, back in the groove. I had to come see bout'cha," Khafre stated, smiling, happy to see another man free.

"Yeah, I been out, like four month's na. Wassup wit'chu doe? I see you in that new Benz electric shit!" Nut said, walking up to Khafre's car to get a better view. "Ya got'cha shortys wit'chi doe?"

"Yeah, I done had two sons. Hassan and Husain. I got one on the way too."

"Damn! I see, you ain't bullshittin'. That's wassup, dow." Nut nodded in approval.

"Respect, respect. Listen doe, I wanted to scream at'cha 'bout somethin'."

"Talk to me," replied Nut, walking back towards his car. Khafre followed Nut to the front of his vehicle.

"Ya fuck wit' that boi?"

"Heroin?" questioned Nut.

"Yeah."

24

"I do my thang, but not down here. I get on that road and go get off in Virginia. Why?" Nut asked, crossing his arms across his chest.

"I got'em for the fifty."

"The whole thang?" Nut questioned, eyebrows raised.

"Yeah."

"That's a damn good price," admitted Nut, rubbing his hand over his beard. "But'chu know I'm Haitian. I got Haitian poppies I'm plugged in wit'. I'm loyal to my people."

"Okay. I can respect that."

"I'ma keep you in mind doe. That's all you got?"

"Heavy artillery."

"Na, see, that's what I'm talkin' about. A nigga can never, have enough guns. What'chu got?" Nut said excitedly.

"State-of-the-art assault rifles."

"What the ticket is?"

"For you—give me four-hundid apiece."

"I call that. Let me get ten of 'em."

"Give me a few days—I'll get'em to ya," Khafre assured.

"A'ight, call me when they ready." They swapped numbers.

"Heeyy, lil' man's! You too young to have on a rollie! Y'all just too cool, huh?" a strange man exclaimed, looking through Khafre's window.

"You know that nigga, Nut?" Khafre asked calmly.

"N'all, I'on know fool."

"Enough said." Khafre drew his pistol and approached the man from the side, who was still peeking through the window.

Crack! Khafre hit the strange man in the left side of his head, dropping him. He then picked the man up by his collar, and pressed his face against the window.

"Look in there! This what'chu wanted, right? Get a good look, stupid ass nigga!" Hassan and Husain had their faces against the window, watching their father perform. Khafre put the pistol to the right side of the man's temple and squeezed one off. *Boc*! Blood and brain matter splattered on the window, before the strange man's body dropped, and everybody scattered. When Khafre looked inside the car, he saw a smile on Husain's face for the first time.

'I'ma catch you later," Nut stated, hopping in his whip. Khafre got in his car and left the scene.

"Y'all okay?" asked Khafre. Husain and Hassan nodded, by way of saying: *Yes*.

"Y'all still want chicken and waffles?"

"Yeesss!" both brothers yelled in unison.

"Okay." Khafre pulled his phone out and dialed out. "Hello?"

"Baby Haitian, wea you at?"

Chapter Five

Fight

Three days later, it was a late summer night on 14th Street. The atmosphere was muggy, and the moon was full. Nut and a few of his homies were pulling an all-nighter, kicking the Bobo and catching money.

"So, you tellin' me, you let that hoe eat'ch yo ass?" Nut asked David, who was the ultimate freak of the bunch.

"Hell yeah, nigga! Yo fuckin' right. I let her clean my shit up. Ya hear me?" David said with no shame.

"Hell nawl!" Nut shrieked, hunched over in laughter.

"You a ole, freaky ass nigga!" added Lee Lee, one of the proficient hustlers of the group.

"What type of time y'all foolz on, my nigga?" Zoe asked, shaking his head odiously as he played in his phone.

"So, she had ja legs in the air and shit?" Nut said, clowning, still laughing.

"She ain't have to, nigga, I had my own shit in the air! Fuck you mean, nigga?" This time everybody doubled over in laughter, clutching their stomachs. "You niggaz sleep! Y'all stuck in that *Stone Age* type fuckin'. Y'all hoez gone be fuckin' wit' David, keep playin'!"

"I ain't fuckin' wit' no hoe who eat ass. I can't do it," stated Nut.

"All dem hoez eat ass, bro," David assured before two known associates rolled up on bikes.

"Wassup, my nigga?" DJ greeted while his partner—Jay—stayed silent.

"Wassup?" Nut replied.

"Where the coke at, my nigga?" asked DJ.

"What'chu want?"

"Let me get a ball."

"I got'cha, come on. Aye, David, we gone finish this conversation when I get back," Nut asserted, walking across the street with DJ behind him. When Nut rounded the Chinese restaurant, he went straight to his bomb that was in a paper bag under a crate. When Nut turned around, DJ had a pistol pointed in his face.

"DJ, what'chu doing?" Nut asked, thinking that DJ was playing.

"You know what it is. Let me get everythang," DJ stated calmly.

"Man, I ain't got nothin'," Nut lied, trying to buy time hoping one of his homies came to check on him.

"You wanna die, nigga? Take that jewelry off. Hurry up." Nut pretended like he was trying to take his rings off. Seeing this, DJ slid his gun back in his jacket. With perfect timing, Nut grabbed DJ, and a tussle ensued.

"Aye! Aye! Y'all niggaz come help me!" Nut yelled, knowing that if he lost his grip around DJ, this would be his last night on earth. Finally, Lee Lee and Zoe rounded the building. David had gone inside the rooming house, so he didn't hear the commotion. As soon as Lee Lee attempted to assist Nut, DJ started shooting through his jacket, hitting Lee Lee in the leg and grazing Nut's finger. Zoe, not wanting to get shot, turned and ran around the Chinese restaurant. Nut finally gathered enough strength to throw DJ to the ground. DJ bounced right up and took off running. *Boc!* A single shot came from behind the Chinese restaurant. Moments later, Zoe came from around the restaurant clutching his abdomen.

"Zoe! Zoe, ya hit?" Nut asked hysterically. Zoe remained silent as he fell into Nut's arms. Zoe and Nut were best friends since snotty noses. "Don't die on me, Zoe! Fight! Fight, Zoe!" Nut cried, tears falling freely from his eyes. Blood poured from Zoe's body, saturating Nut's clothing.

"Come on, man, Zoe! Fight! Fight, Zoe!" Nut pleaded but Zoe was gone.

***

When Ketta entered the hotel room, she was surprised to find it swimming in a sea of endless roses. Red long-stemmed roses covered every possible inch of space, from the floor, table, the top of the TV, and the bed. Khafre laid naked in an ocean of rose petals, with an erection, and the stem of a rose between his teeth while bearing a wicked smile.

"What the fuck is all this?" Ketta smiled. "Boy, yo' ass, is crazy," asserted Ketta, enthralled. She had never experienced real intimacy with a man. Only rough sex and fly-by- nights; so, the romanticism that Khafre was displaying was foreign to her. Khafre remained silent, and jerked his head backwards, instructing her to come closer. Ketta dropped her Fendi bag on the floor, loosened her matching trench coat and let it slip from her shoulders, falling next to her bag. In an instant, the room grew hot and steamy, with the threat of sex. All she wore was a laced teddy and an extremely expensive pair of Saint Laurent heels. As she moved towards the bed, Khafre used his right arm to sweep away a clearing for her, causing roses to fly across the room. Ketta slid beside Khafre, but he still said nothing. He hovered over her sinisterly as she leaned back into the butter-soft pillows.

"You bought all these roses for me?" Ketta asked, but received no answer. Khafre removed the rose from between his teeth and traced it down the center of her forehead, lightly past her nose, over the swells of her succulent lips, and snaked a trail down her neck, barely grazing her skin. Ketta found the sensation electric. Khafre gazed into her eyes, as he slipped the teddy delicately off her shoulders, and down her waist. Ketta pushed it all the way down, raising her ass so it could pass, and letting it linger around her knees. Placing her butt back on the bed, a thorny-stemmed rose punctured her ass. Caught off guard, she was instantly wet. Pain and pleasure was everything to Ketta. Khafre swirled the rose around her perfect size nipples, then placed his mouth on each one. He sucked, kissed, licked, then blew softly on each nipple, causing Ketta to gasp, closing her eyes. A tender kiss on her lips caused her eyes to open. She had never been kissed by anyone outside of relationships. Petal to skin, Khafre began to trace a deeper descent down her body with the rose. When he reached her clit, he stopped and made circular motions around the hood of it. Khafre used his left forefinger to pull it back, exposing her clit to the now bruised surface of the rose petals. He then twirled and stroked her clit with the rose, while staring in her eyes.

"Damn, that shit feels good," Ketta whispered. She tried to say something else, but Khafre vetoed that by placing his mouth over hers. As he kissed her skillfully, all she wanted or could think about was Khafre's dick.

"I'm so fuckin' wet," Ketta moaned, throwing and grinding her hips. Khafre ignored her remark and rubbed the rose down the side of her lower lips. The petals made her labia tingle, giving off a strange sensation. Ketta pressed her pelvis up against the rose, crushing it between her legs as they scissored shut. Khafre roughly spread her legs apart, noting that the ruined rose was now drenched in Ketta's pussy juice.

"Fuck me, nigga, shit!" Ketta cried out of lust in response to an itch that desperately needed scratching. She reached for Khafre's dick, which was rock solid and attempted to guide him to her love flower. He allowed the tip of his dick to touch the entrance of her pussy, then pulled back. Ketta wanted to come so bad that she could barely breathe. Khafre lowered himself and faced off with her pussy. It was the prettiest pussy he'd ever laid eyes on. Khafre blew lightly on her clit, and to her own surprise, she came. Heat filled her walls, causing ultra-strong spasms. Ketta moaned heavily and collapsed. Khafre smiled wickedly as her thighs trembled much too hard to form words.

"You ain't ready for this shit," Khafre stated, climbing out of the bed to get dressed.

"Sss—Whhhoooo—Shit! Sss—wait. Please. Whhhooo—please. Sshit. Ss—please don't leave," begged Ketta.

Khafre ignored her and headed outside, closing the door behind him. Moments later, Ketta snatched the door open and was startled by Khafre's presents. Before she could speak, he grabbed her by the throat and forced her back into the room, closing the door behind him.

"You thought that shit was cute the other night, huh!" Khafre said, roughly throwing Ketta on the bed. She said nothing as her heart rate increased, curious as to what was to come. Khafre grabbed two pillows, and snatched the pillow cases off.

"Turn yo' thick ass around!" he demanded.

"Ummm," moaned Ketta, as she did as she was told. Khafre straddled Ketta's back and tied a pillow case around her mouth.

"You have the right to remain silent." Khafre grabbed her hands and tied them behind her back with the other pillow case.

"Anything you say can and will be held against yo' pussy!" Khafre's role playing created an intense tingling deep within the walls of her pussy. She exhaled deeply as she placed her head down, ass up, and began to sway from side to side. *Smack*!

"Who told yo' ass to move?" Khafre questioned, removing his designer sweatpants. "Stop resisting!" *Smack*!

He smacked Ketta on her ass again with more force, drawing a long muffled groan. Khafre entered her from behind with ease. He pushed deep within her pussy and held it there. Ketta climaxed instantly and clenched around Khafre's shaft.

"Who told you to cum? You leave me no choice but to use lethal force on that ass!" Khafre grabbed Ketta's ponytail like a rein, and rode her like a thoroughbred.

"Ummmm! Ummmm!" Ketta moaned muffled sounds of pain and bliss while her vagina made sounds that sounded like extra cheesy pasta being stirred. *Smack!* Khafre slapped Ketta's ass with extreme pressure, causing her to groan loader.

"You ain't gone pull no moe niggaz over when you out there in the field, is you?" *Smack!*

"Ummmm—Grrrr!"

"I can't fuckin' hear you!" *Smack!* Khafre could feel her climaxing for the third time.

"Bitch! Who told you to cum without permission?" Khafre stopped stroking her and removed the pillow case that was tied around her head and mouth.

"You a rebellious one, huh?"

"Sss—Whooooo—shit! Nigga, fuck you!" Ketta retorted while her pussy muscles contracted around Khafre's dick.

"Fuck me, huh? A'ight!" Khafre pulled out of her and used the juices from her sodden pussy to lubricate her ass. He then put his right foot on the left side of her face, navigated his dick to her asshole, and squatted down on her.

"Haaaah, God!"

"Umm-hmm!" Khafre taunted as he began to rock back in forth. He dubbed this position "The Surf Board."

"Ooowww, fuck! Sss—Aaaaahh! Okay, nigga, fuck! O-fff-shh-shhit! Okay—I'm—sor—aaaah! Sorry!"

"Yeah, I know you is, bitch! You gone move daddy dope?"

"Whooooo—yeah, yeah! I'ma—I'ma do it, daddy!"

"That's a good girl! Na, take this wit'cha!" Khafre took his foot off of her head, straddled her and fucked her ass until he came.

"Whooooooo! Fuck! Yes, nigga cum in this ass!" Ketta cried as she came from her pussy and ass simultaneously. Khafre growled like a Presa Canario as he unloaded in her. When he released everything in him, he pulled out of her aggressively and headed straight to the shower.

Ketta moaned, hugging a pillow. She was asleep within moments.

When Khafre returned from the bathroom, his phone rang. He glanced at Ketta before sitting at the foot of the bed, then answered his phone.

"Yeah?"

"What's good, bro? This Nut." Khafre could hear the pain in Nut's voice.

"Talk to me."

"I'ma need what I asked you for, a lil' faster than a few dayz."

"How soon?"

"Like, right na."

Chapter Six

No Police

Nut and Zoe had been best friends since elementary, so it was hard for him to face Zoe's mother. As much as he feared the worst, she surprisingly took the death of her son well. There was no wailing, just memories of her last moments with her son, and cascading tears. Zoe's mom knew the relationship that Nut and Zoe had, so she was content with knowing that Nut would never intentionally put her son in harm's way. She embraced Nut, wrapped her arms around his neck and began to speak Creole into his ear.

"*Mwen pa vle enplike lapolis la, e mwen vle ou vanje pitit gason m 'lan.*"

"*Mwen konprann,*" replied Nut, kissing Mama Zoe on her cheek before walking outside to let her words sink in. Mama Zoe had just told Nut that she didn't want to involve the police, and that she wanted him to avenge her son. Nut assured her he understood. Nut was in deep thought formulating a plan, when Lee Lee and David approached him.

"Nut, this shit, all yo' fault, my nigga," voiced David.

"It is, man. All you had to do was give that shit up. Ya could have got all that shit back, nigga. We can't get Zoe back, Nut," Lee Lee added.

"What! I was supposed to just, let a nigga take my shit? How the fuck I knew Zoe was gone get killed? Them niggaz ain't have no mask on, they was gone kill one of us, anyway!" Nut emphasized.

"You don't know that, Nut," David countered.

"Man, y'all niggaz gone sit around and keep blaming me or y'all gone retaliate? That's what I wanna know, kuz blaming me ain't gone bring Zoe back. Y'all know everybody don't like us Haitians, so some shit like this was gone happen, anyway! Na, wassup? You niggaz gone cry or ride?"

"We already been spinnin', lookin for that nigga DJ and Jay. We can't find them niggaz nowhere," asserted David. Nut rubbed his hand over his beard.

"That nigga Jay gotta brother who be rappin' and shit, right?" questioned Nut.

"Yeah. You talkin' bout that nigga KJ," Lee Lee replied.

"What about that nigga?" asked David.

"Go in the house and get Lil' Haiti," Nut instructed Lee Lee. Moments later, Lee Lee returned with Lil' Haiti.

"That nigga KJ still wanna do a song wit'chu?"

"Yeah, he been on my line. Why? Wassup?"

"Wait a few days, then hit'em up. Start taking him to the studio. I'll take it from there."

"Say no moe," exclaimed Lil' Haiti.

***

It was fifteen minutes after three a.m. when Nut left Mama Zoe's house. He rode in silence as the vision of Zoe's last moments kept replaying in his mind, along with mama Zoe's wishes. As soon as Nut made a right on 14th and Canal, he saw police lights in his rearview.

"Ahh, shit. The fuck these pussy ass crakaz pulling me over for?" Nut muttered to himself. He felt like taking 'em on a high speed chase just for the fuck of it but decided against it. He was clean anyway. Once Nut was pulled over, the police killed the lights on the cruiser, and stepped out. Nut observed the officer approaching with her hand on her service weapon, and thought that maybe this could be his last moment on earth.

"Kill the engine, and place your hands out of the window, now!" the officer demanded. Nut did as he was told. He then made a mental note that nobody else was around. No humans or stray animals, just him and the officer.

"You mind tellin' me why you pulled me, officer." Nut implored.

"Yeah, you was swerving. Have you been drinking?"

"I don't drink, officer."

"License and registration."

"I'ma reach for it, don't shoot me."

"Go ahead." Nut reached slowly, grabbed his information and handed it to the officer.

"Sit tight." The officer headed to her cruiser and checked Nut's information. She then popped her trunk, got out and headed towards Nut.

"Pop your trunk for me please."

"For what, officer?"

"Not gone ask you again." Nut sucked his teeth then popped his trunk. The officer headed back to her cruiser, grabbed two duffle bags and placed them in Nut's trunk. She then handed Nut back his license and registration.

"Ya free to go."

"Oh hell nawl! What'chu put in my trunk, lady?"

"That's a gift from Khafre. He said to call him if you need him. You have a good night," Ketta said, then headed back to her cruiser and pulled off.

"A gift from Khafre?" Nut muttered. He popped the trunk then got out to survey what was placed in his trunk. When he unzipped the duffles, he viewed ten state-of-the-art assault rifles.

"Da fuck? This nigga Khafre, hell!"

Chapter Seven

You Wanna Live?

It was a nippy summer night about fifteen after twelve a.m. The moon was full, stars innumerable, and the streets desolate. Everything seemed to be falling in place for KJ. He'd recorded numerous tracks, a buzz was being created, and he had shows lined up. The feeling was nostalgic.

"I'm tellin' you, my nigga! Deez niggaz can't fuck wit' me on this music tip, no capp! And dey hoes on my top!" KJ boasted as he mobbed down 14th and Canal.

"You be doin' ya thang, bra. Once that shit in you it can't be denied, my nigga. You on yo' way," Tim declared, stroking KJ's ego.

"Yeah, you already know how this shit go. On another note, doe, wassup wit' deez hoez we finna go see?" inquired KJ.

"Oh, deez lil' hoes some eaterz! Dey all da way live!"

"Deez hoez ain't fat, is'a?"

"I know mine ain't. I'on know 'bout 'urs, but if she is, you gotta take one for the team," Tim said, laughing.

"If she fat, ain't no dope. I'm sliding," KJ replied, shaking his head. Tim continued to laugh before replying.

"N'all, my girl say she bad. Say she gotta fat azz, and she a yellow bone."

"Okay, that's most definitely a vibe. I'ma beat her back in."

"Wassup, nigga?" a voice interjected from behind KJ and Tim. When the duo turned around, they were surprised to see Nut and Moe dipped in all-black. Nut stood tough while Moe pointed a .40 in KJ's face. KJ stood frozen in despair, already knowing why he was staring down the barrel of a gun.

"I ain't have nothing to do wit' Zoe gettin' killed, man," pleaded KJ. With a nod of Nut's head, Moe squeezed one off, hitting KJ in the head. His soul was lifted before his body hit the dirt road in an awkward position. Tim backpedaled aghast with his hands in the air trembling.

"Wassup, nigga? You wanna live?" Nut asked in a collected tone that Tim found terrifying. He nodded, his head going up and down in a frenzy.

"Yeah, man, I ain't see shit," Tim retorted, his voice crackling.

"You trippin', let me hit this nigga," Moe pleaded.

"N'all, let the nigga live. I know where his mama stay. Come on," Nut pronounced and jogged off. Moe looked at Tim one last time before taking off behind Nut. Once he rounded a few apartments, he saw the getaway car and hopped in.

"Y'all wiped his nose?" Khafre asked, pulling off.

"Yeah, we good," Nut assured.

"Why you let the nigga live?" Moe questioned.

"Man, shut the fuck up! He ain't a threat. We got who we came for."

"This shit gone come back on us, man," cried Moe.

"What he hollin' 'bout?" Khafre said.

"It ain't nothin', trust me," Nut assured. "Moe, chill the fuck out!" Moe hissed like a snake and gazed out of the window in disbelief.

***

Three Weeks Later—

Thank you for using Global Tel Link You have a pre-paid call from Moe. To accept press—" Nut accepted the call.

"What's goin' on?" Nut asked.

"Maan, crakaz picked me up," replied Moe bitterly.

"What the charge is?"

"They picked me up for murder. Man I told–" *Click*! Nut hung the phone up and threw it out the window.

"Wassup, bra?" questioned Khafre

"Krakaz picked Moe up. This nigga on the phone talkin' crayz knowin' that shit being recorded."

"What he said?"

"Shid, I ain't give 'em a chance."

"You think he gone fold?"

"N'all, he ain't gone say nothin'," assured Nut.

"You should have killed that nigga Tim, bra. You know how this shit go."

"I know. His mama was the candy lady and shit. We grew up together, so I tried to spare the nigga." Khafre shook his head in disagreement. Nut rubbed his hand over his beard before speaking.

"Take me to 12th Street," requested Nut. Three minutes later they were on 12th and Avenue H. "Pull in right there, bra." Khafre pulled in front of an apartment and put the car in *park*.

"Who stay here?"

"The nigga Tim mama stay here."

"You think he in there?" Asked Khafre

"N'all, he don't live here."

"So what'chu gone do? Talk to his mama?" Khafre questioned with raised eyebrows.

"I was hoping you do it for me," Nut admitted with pleading eyes. Khafre glanced at Nut dubiously.

"Why me?"

"Kuz she don't know you. And she is like a mother to me." Khafre took a moment to consider. After thinking it over, he realized that he was the getaway driver, which made him an accessory to murder. If Moe folded under pressure, shit would be bad for all parties. He couldn't fathom losing his sons.

"A'ight," Khafre agreed.

"All you gotta do is talk to her," assured Nut.

"A'ight. She still the candy lady?"

"Yeah."

"I got it," Khafre replied, then stepped out of his car and headed to the front door. After knocking on the door three times, Ms. Bertha opened the door.

"How you doing, young man? Can I help you?" Ms. Bertha asked in the sweetest voice.

"I'm doing fine, ma'am. And yes I was hoping that maybe you could help me. Would you happen to have any pickled sausage, or homemade pickled eggs?" Khafre asked as civil as possible.

"Yes, I have both. You may come in," Ms. Bertha offered, standing to the side to let Khafre in. After closing the door, she headed to the kitchen with Khafre behind her.

"How many you want, young man?" Bertha asked, grabbing sandwich bags.

"Four of each, ma'am," said Khafre, surveying the home.

"You can just call me, Ms. Bertha," she replied, chuckling.

"Okay, Ms. Bertha." She sat the sausages and eggs on the table.

"That'll be five dollars." Bertha said with one hand on her hip.

"Ms. Bertha. Would you by any chance happen to know where your son—Tim—is?" Khafre asked, reaching in his pocket.

"No, baby. I haven't seen Tim in a few weeks. Why? Is it anything you want me to tell 'em?"

"Yes, ma'am." Khafre drew a compact .40 from his right pocket and pointed in Bertha's face. Bertha gasped before speaking.

"Lord Jesus!" cried Bertha, putting her hand over her mouth.

"Listen to me, and hear me correctly. You tell yo' ungrateful ass son to recant his statement, or make arrangements to bury his mother." Bertha listened intently before replying.

"What is this about?" Bertha questioned, emphasizing with her hands.

"He knows," Khafre retorted briskly, slapping her across her nose with the pistol. Blood splattered about the kitchen before she slumped down. Her wailing didn't stop Khafre's onslaught. He swiped his pistol across her face five more times, breaking her jaw and nose.

"Tell yo son, he better develop amnesia, or a closer relationship wit' God. Kuz if I gotta come back, I'm lifting souls into the unknown." Khafre grabbed the pickled eggs and sausages then made his way outside. Once in the car, Nut gazed at Khafre dubiously.

"What happen?"

"I talked to her," replied Khafre, pulling off.

"And?"

"She gone make sho' he do what's right for both parties."

"How you know?" Nut questioned, wanting to know all the details.

"Pickled sausage or pickled egg?" Khafre offered Nut. Nut grabbed the bag and noticed blood splatter all over it. He looked at Khafre knowingly but still asked:

"Maan, what'chu dun did to Ms. Bertha?"

Chapter Eight

Too Much Blood

Three Years Later—

Khafre sat at a cherry oak table and fed his two-year-old daughter. Quen had given birth to a beautiful little girl that Khafre named Assata.

"Tell me the size of the human heart," Khafre inquired, feeding Assata fruits.

"The heart is five inches in length and three inches in diameter," Hassan answered quickly.

"That's correct. Husain, how many times the heart beats within a minute?"

"I'on feel like talkin' about this, dad. I wanna play the video game," cried Husain.

"I'ma ask ya ass one more time, boy," Khafre stated warily.

Husain drew in a lot of air before answering.

"Seventy-two times a minute, forty-two hundred times an hour, one-hundred-thousand and eight-hundred times a day and twenty-six million, seven-hundred twenty-five thousand, two hundred times a year."

"Hassan, how many pounds does the brain weigh?"

"Three!"

"What is wrong wit'chu?" Quen questioned. "These kids are only six years old. Why are you asking them such difficult questions?" Quen sat two bowls of salad on the table for Husain and Hassan.

"Don't touch that food," exclaimed Khafre, stopping his sons in mid-reach of the bowls.

"Are you serious?" Quen questioned.

"I'ma tell you this shit, one time, and one time only. Don't ever tell me how to raise my kids. Ever!" Quen was startled by Khafre's aggressiveness. "All my years in school, I didn't have not one teacher who taught me shit that was relevant to real life. I'm not having that shit wit' my sons or my daughter. Home schooling is what it is. You gotta problem wit' that?" Quen shook her head, by way of saying: *No.*

"I didn't mean to upset you, baby. I'm sorry."

"You good."

"Can I have Assata?" Quen asked after apologizing to Khafre.

"Yeah," said Khafre, lifting Assata out of her high chair. He placed a kiss on her cheek, and handed her to Quen.

"I'ma be in the room if you need me, baby," stated Quen, walking off.

"Now, which one of y'all can tell me what it means to be *black*?" Hassan raised his hand.

"Hassan, go 'head."

"Um—to be black means to be first," answered Hassan.

"What'chu mean? Explain."

"To be black means to be the fathers of humanity," Hassan said.

"What is humanity?"

"Humanity is man and mankind."

"What's the difference between man and mankind?"

"Um—man is the black people, like me, and mankind is the white people like mommy," Hassan said, throwing Khafre off a little.

"What'chu mean, Hassan, Quen is black."

"I know," said Hassan. "I'm talking about my other mommy," he added.

"That's correct. Y'all gon eat'cha food now," Khafre asserted, changing the subject. Moments later his phone rang.

"Y'all eat up." Khafre got up and headed out back.

"Yeah, wassup?" answered Khafre.

"What's goin' on, family man?" asked Nut.

"You already know, vibin' wit' my younginz. What up? You a'ight?"

"Yeah, I'm good. You seen the paper?"

"N'all, wassup?"

"The nigga, Moe, beat the murder charge."

"Oh yeah?"

"Yeah, man, I'm so glad that shit over wit'. That nigga was in there trippin!" Nut explained.

"Don't do nothin' else wit' that nigga, man."

"I know right," Nut agreed, laughing. "Listen though, man. I'm finna get on that road, and hit Virginia. I can't get in touch wit' my people, man. You still got that pedigree?"

"Yeah, when you leaving?"

"Soon as possible," Nut said.

"Give me a few hours," stated Khafre, walking to his bar and fixing a shot.

"A'ight, just hit me."

"Already!" *Click!* Khafre hung the phone up and dialed Wolly's line. He picked up on the third ring.

"Khafre, buddy! How are you, my friend?"

"Ock! I need to see you," said Khafre, downing a shot of Remy.

"Come! I'm here, buddy."

"A'ight, I'm in ya chest in a few minutes," Khafre assured.

"In my chest? How do you mean?" Khafre laughed.

"I'm on the way, ock." *Click!*

44

***

After locking the store up, Wolly took Khafre into his hidden man cave, handed him a Cuban cigar, and poured shots of fifteen-year-aged blended Scotch whisky. Both men downed their shots then put flame to their cigars.

"So my friend, how's business?" Wolly said in his strong Islamic accent.

"Bidness is fruitful. Actually that's why I'm here," said Khafre, pouring another shot.

"What is it?" Wolly asked, blowing smoke in the air.

"I need ten of 'em."

"How come you never go above ten?" Wolly was curious.

"I'm kool wit' ten, Wolly, I'on need all that shit. I make a quick mill and shoot'chu five-hunid. I'm still seein' bank."

"You should go big. Big risk, big reward," Wolly preached.

"Right na, I'm good."

"Okay, buddy. Your call." Wolly took a pull from his cigar before speaking again. "Have you seen newspaper?" Wolly asked, grabbing the paper.

"N'all, wassup?" Wolly handed Khafre the paper.

"Maybe selling assault rifles was bad idea. You should keep all weapons for self. You people are spilling too much blood. Violence brings heat. City now crawling with cops." Wolly fixed another shot of whiskey as he waited for a response. Khafre viewed the paper and saw the body count in the last two months. All the murders were taking place in the areas he did business in.

"Don't worry yaself, ock. I'ma take care of it," Khafre assured.

"Okay. I trust you will. Load ten cans in garbage bag, and take back door to your apartment."

"A'ight, ock," Khafre responded, pulling out his phone and dialing out.

"Hey, daddy!" greeted Ketta cheerfully.

"I need you to deliver somethin' to Nut for me."

"No problem, daddy."

"Meet me at the spot."

"On my way." *Click!*

Chapter Nine

Sit Down

It was a jovial summer day in Port St. Lucie. The sun was out but a soothing breeze still pervaded the atmosphere, causing palm trees to sway gently. Khafre had rented an Airbnb to have a sit-down with all the OG's in the city who controlled the areas he supplied. Seated at the head of a twenty-foot granite table, with Ketta standing to the right of him in civilian clothes, Khafre ran down the discrepancies and gave solutions.

"Somebody wanna tell me why the fuck all this blood being spilt? Huh? Everybody eatin', so it can't be a monetary issue. And if it is monetary somebody gettin' stepped on, cause I'on tolerate that greed shit. Make me feel like you lookin' at my plate next." An OG from 10th Street named LBG drew in a lot of air and exhaled seethingly.

"What up, LB? You a'ight?" Khafre questioned warily.

"Tsss." LBG shook his head from left to right stolidly before replying.

"Maan, you know exactly how I'm comin'," LBG stated, causing Khafre to snicker.

"Oh yeah? A'ight, homie. Anybody else gotta lil' tension?"

An OG named Lloyd from 113th spoke up. "I'ma keep it real wit'chu, my nigga. The blood that's being spilt today results from blood spilt in the past. This shit go back, generations my nigga. It's niggaz in here right na done killed some of my people, I done flipped a few of their people. This shit deep, my nigga," exclaimed Lloyd.

"A'ight. I here what'chu sayin', my nigga. I'ma street nigga, so I can identify wit' that. But, if this shit that deep, why y'all ain't in here squeezin' off shots? Huh? When it's up there, it's stuck there, ana?"

"You know, I fuck wit'chu, Khafre," Lloyd admitted. The only reason I ain't line one of these niggas up is kuz of you."

"You just rappin, nigga," T-Byrd from the projects interjected.

"Come on, man. I done caught'chu slippin' plenty times, nigga, I be sparing you," replied Lloyd.

"All y'all know wassup wit' me. Duce Trey, nigga," added Tay from 23rd Street.

"Aye! Y'all calm all that shit down! Got the city hot over nothin'! Y'all don't know why y'all killin' each other, kuz you wasn't born when this shit started. Y'all niggaz movin' off pride and ego. Emotions and shit, half the time over a bitch," Khafre shook his head in disgust. "Listen, this what it is. Y'all gone cease fire, and get this money. Anybody gotta issue wit' that, I ain't supplying ya ass no moe. The work I was frontin' you—I'ma give it to one of ya lil' homies to step on ya. That's just what's going on. Speak na, if you don't like it," declared Khafre. A few OG's posture denoted anger, but they said nothin'.

"Man, a nigga don't need you," LBG stated, flashing a devilish grin. "I been gettin' money out'chere, playboy."

"You fearless, I admire that. Anybody else?" Silence cut through the ambience like butter as the other OG's sat amicably. It was hard to find a heroin plug as pure as Khafre's in the city. Khafre's numbers were better and he fronted the work, so the OG's fell in compliance. "Well, it's stamped then. A cease fire been stipulated."

Khafre looked at LBG square in the eye. "LBG, that debt you owe me been cleared. Get the fuck out!" demanded Khafre. Ketta followed behind him to make sure he found his way out. When she came back, Khafre made her pour shots of a fifteen-hundred-dollar bottle of eighteen-year-old Yamazaki. She then placed a brick by every OG at the table which was seven in total.

"Glasses in the air," ordered Khafre. Everybody followed suit. "In life, if you don't risk anything, you risk everythang! I salute you OG's for putin' ya pride to the side, for the bigger picture. Salute!"

"Salute!" everybody screamed in unison.

***

"Ssss—oooww—Fuck yeah! Beat that pussy, nigga!" Ketta moaned as she sat in her unmarked vehicle playing in her pussy. She was watching a *West Coast* production that displayed Rico fucking Cherokee and Pinky at the same time.

"Ummm—that's right, nut on that dick—sss—sshit! I'm cumin'—sss—Aaahh! Ummm! Oooww, yes!" Ketta cried, cumin' all over her fingers. When she was finished, she licked her fingers clean, then focused her mind back on her mark. Ketta had just made detective, and was on a stake out. She was backed in next to a small restaurant on 39th and Louisiana, watching an apartment complex across the street. As soon as she lit a Newport, her mark came out of his apartment, hopped in an Infinity and pulled off. The moment Ketta pulled behind the mark, he spotted her, and quickly made a left on a dirt road that was a dead end. Ketta called it in, then cut her lights on and pulled the Infinity over. She hopped out brusquely, and approached the vehicle with her hand on her service weapon. The driver let the window down, allowing the stench of weed and liquor to exit his vehicle.

"What's the problem, officer?"

"You failed to use your turning signal. You mind tellin' me where you're headed so late in the night?"

"Yeah, I'm just headed to Wal-Mart to get some formula for my daughter, ma'am."

"Walmart is the other way, sir," Ketta retorted.

"I know. Before you pulled me, I was just making a U-turn," replied the driver, now recognizing who Ketta was. "Don't I know you?" he questioned as his phone began to ring.

"Hands off the gun!"

Boc!

Boc!

Boc!

Ketta put two slugz in LBG's chest, and one in his head. Khafre had ordered Ketta to lay on him and wipe his nose as soon as the opportunity presented itself.

Chapter Ten

Beer Man

It was 27 degrees in Winchester, Virginia. Nut was on Kent Kern St, posted on the block in a bubble goose jacket, dickies, and a pair of Retro 5 Air Jordans, getting money. Knowing how uptown niggaz get down, Nut had linked with a few down south homies who were already in Virginia getting money. Ricardo, Lee, and Moe were in front of Smitty's pool hall while Nut caught his money. They all took turns catching plays, and never fought over customers. It was enough for everybody.

"Maan, that white bitch crazy, man," Nut stated, putting the money he'd just made in his pocket.

"What happened?" Ricardo asked, taking a toke from a blunt.

"This bitch offered her fifteen-year-old daughter to me for a gram," Nut said in disgust.

"What'chu told her?" Lee questioned, grabbing the blunt from Ricardo.

"Fuck you think I told her? Told that bitch, quit playin' wit' me and come off that paper."

"That dog food serious," voiced Ricardo, referring to heroin. Another customer came to cop, and it was Ricardo's turn, so he walked off to catch'em. Moe was on his phone conversing with a chick he'd met since being in Virginia. Almost every dollar he made went to his new love—Jenny.

"Look at this nigga, Moe! You don't wanna do nothin', but be up under Jenny all damn day. I know that's who you in ya phone textin'. You barely even wanna get money, you so pussy-whipped! How you gone keep the bitch, if you focused on her all the time instead of the money? You know the bitch love money," Nut clowned and laughed mirthlessly.

"She ain't no bitch, man," Moe replied, irritation in his tone.

Lee laughed.

"All man, outta everything I said, that's what'chu got from that?" Lee continued to laugh.

"She ain't no bitch, bra," Moe repeated this time, voice deep and cruel.

"All lawd! Na, you wanna kill me 'bout this hoe! This shit, crazy!"

Moe's eyes were now smoldering with hatred, when Ricardo made haste towards them.

"Beer Man coming up the street on foot," Ricardo informed, which prompted everybody to walk inside of Smitty's pool hall. Smitty was behind a wall that had a window in it, that he used to serve beer and hot wings out of. Everybody quickly handed their drugs and money to Smitty, who put them in a safe. He took a small percentage every time this happened. Nut quickly sent a text from his phone, then grabbed a pool stick. Moments later, Beer Man, who was a vicious dick head cop, entered the pool hall. Everybody remained reserved and collected, while shooting pool. This rubbed Beer Man the wrong way because he'd just seen Ricardo catch a sale. He wanted his palms greased.

"Very comical. Okay, motherfuckers, up against the wall!" ordered Beer Man.

Everybody lined up on the wall with no argument.

"Where ya back up?" Nut asked. Beer Man laughed satanically.

"I'ma one-man fucking army, dude. Who needs back up for a couple of minions?" Beer Man inquired while searching Nut.

"Man, who you think you talkin' to?" Nut said.

"Nut, shut up man," cried Moe.

52

"Don't tell 'em nothing," said Beer Man, searching Ricardo. "Where's the fucking money?" asked Beer Man.

"What money?" Ricardo retorted.

"Motherfucker, I just seen you make a sale."

"You ain't see me do shit! I gave that lady my last five dollars."

"Don't fucking bullshit me!"

"A'ight! That's enough of that shit! You've searched them boys and they're clean! Get the fuck outta my establishment unless you gotta warrant!" Smitty announced, voice thickening with menace.

"You can bet your ass I'll be back with one!"

"Well, I damn sho' ain't betting no ass but'cha can bet shit gone get sticky, if you don't leave my place of bidness. Harassing folk," exclaimed Smitty, clutching his .357 Magnum behind the wall.

"You making threats to a police officer?"

"A crooked one, yeah! Now get the fuck out!"

"Okay, Mr. Smitty. I'll be back," Beer Man assured, backing out of the pool hall. Everybody quickly approached Smitty for their drugs and money.

"A'ight, that's a hundred dollars each," asserted Smitty. Everybody thanked Smitty, paid him and stepped out of the pool hall. Everybody hopped in their cars except Nut. He didn't want his ride at the spot, so he parked it at Ashanti's house. Nut had met Ashanti through Moe's girl, Jenny. They were very close but their relationship was strictly platonic. All Nut wanted was the money. Ashanti was outside waiting on Nut. He hopped in and headed to her house.

***

Nut was seated at the kitchen table devouring a plate of Haitian Griot and plantains when Ashanti took a seat across from him. She opened a bottle of Moscoto, and took a sip before speaking.

"Nut, I forgot to tell you my sister and her boyfriend are on their way down here from DC. She said, Ox wanted a nine-piece," Ashanti said, taking another sip of wine. Nut sat his spoon down with a dubious expression.

"Ain't nobody call me and said shit. How she even know that I'm up here?" How she know if I got work or not?" Nut questioned, picking his spoon back up and stuffing his face.

"Come on, Nut, if you up here, you got work. That's the only reason you come up here."

"It don't matter, Ashanti, don't be doing that shit. You know I'on like dealing wit' them D.C. niggaz like that," Nut said, slightly agitated.

"Yeah, but you already did business with Ox. You know he good peoples. Come on, Nut, just do it for me, please," Ashanti begged, smiling.

"Maan! How close they is?"

"They should be pulling up any minute now."

"You got'em pullin' up here?"

"Yeah."

"Why would you tell them to come here, where the work at? I'ma have to meet them at Smitty's or somewhere else." Ashanti's phone rang.

"Hello?" answered Ashanti. "Okay." *Click!* "They outside."

Nut shook his head in disappointment.

"For you to love your daughter as much as you do, you sho'll be moving reckless." There was a knock at the door.

"That's my sister, Nut. She wouldn't put her niece in harm's way," Ashanti assured before walking off to open the door.

"Heeyy, sis!" Kimbella greeted, hugging Ashanti's neck.

"Hey, girl," said Ashanti. Ox entered the home behind Kimbella with an unfamiliar face with him.

"Ox, who is this nigga?" questioned Ashanti.

"This my cousin, Worm. Relax, slim, he good," Ox said. Nut didn't acknowledge Ox or his cousin, Worm. Instead he continued to enjoy his Haitian dish.

"Wassup, beloved?" Ox greeted Nut, walking towards the table. Nut nodded, and continued to eat his food. "Food gotta be good, you can't even talk, huh, slim?" Ox made his way around the table.

"Wat'chu got there, slim?" asked Ox, looking over Nut's food.

"Aye, man, wait in the living room. I'ma see you in a minute," Nut stated.

"A'ight, slim," Ox replied, pulling a Springfield .45 from his North Face jacket, and pointing it in Nut's face. "Run that shit, slim!"

"What the fuck is you doing?" asked Kimbella.

"Yeah, nigga, what the fuck is wrong with you?" Ashanti added.

"Both of you bitches, shut the fuck up and lay down," Worm demanded, pulling his 9mm. Both women had laid face down in the living room.

"Run that shit, slim!" ordered Ox again. Nut started to buck the jack, but thought about what happened to Zoe when he did last time. *Smack!* Ox hit Nut in the side of his head with the pistol for stalling.

"You wanna die, slim?"

"Better talk fast. You gone fuck around and get these bitches smoked too," threatened Worm.

"No, please, my daughter is upstairs," cried Ashanti.

"Oh yeah?" asked Worm. "Let me go see how she's doing."

"A'ight, man, it's under the couch," Nut finally admitted.

"Worm, get the work," Ox stated. Worm moved swiftly and quickly found 18 ounces of heroin.

"Got it, let's roll out," said Worm.

"I should line you up, slim. Today's your lucky day," said Ox, backing up cautiously. "Kimbella, your services are no longer needed. Thanks for the line-up." Ox smirked satanically before him and Worm backed out of the house and disappeared into the night. Nut stared at Ashanti and Kimbella with blood in his eyes.

Chapter Eleven

City of No Pity

"One, two, side step, right hook! One, two, side step, right hook! That's what the fuck I'm talkin' 'bout! Husain, boy you lookin' like Shakur Stevenson out this motherfucka!" Khafre said as his phone began to ring. He eyed it and saw that it was Nut calling.

"A'ight, Hassan, you next up. Get'cha ass in there!" Hassan stepped up and immediately peppered the heavy bag with proficient combinations.

"Stay on ya toe! Hello, what up?" answered Khafre.

"What's goin' on, mane?" asked Nut soberly.

"In my backyard under my pavilion training my boyz. You a'ight? You sound peevish."

"Who?"

"You sound irritated. What up?"

"Maan, some niggaz from D.C. robbed me."

"Damn! How you get caught lackin'?"

"I was doin' a favor for this hoe people and the niggaz got me."

"So the hoe lined you up?"

"Not intentionally. You know how them hoez is, mane. She was just tryin' to do a favor for her sister's boyfriend. They ain't have nothin' to do wit' it. Them niggaz acted alone."

"You better than me. I would have made them hoez a plate."

"What'chu mean?" Nut asked, confused.

"I woulda ate'em."

Nut chuckled, before responding.

"Nall, they good people. They just blind to a lot of street shit."

"I guess, man. So what up? What's next?"

"I'ma send my people to holla at'chu. Them niggaz ain't do shit but piss me off," Nut retorted with a snake-like suavity.

"What they hit'chu for?"

"Eighteen."

"You need me to pull up?"

"N'all, I got it. You know these up north niggaz think we country and slow as fuck," Nut laughed. "I'ma sho'em how dirty the *City of no Pity* gets."

"A'ight, do you. Just have ya people pull up on 114th Street. I'ma get it to'em."

"A'ight, bra, love."

"Already!"

***

It was a beautiful clear summer night in Virginia. The day had been very fruitful for all parties at Smitty's pool hall, and now Ricardo, Lee, and Moe were trying to get Nut to go out to a club.

"Maan, y'all niggaz trippin'! I ain't came up here to risk my life for this money, just to blow it in the club. That shit don't add up," stated Nut gravely.

"Yo', tight ass! You can't take this shit to the grave, nigga," Ricardo added.

"I'ma be the first nigga to do it," clowned Nut.

"Come on, Nut man, let's hang out," said Moe.

"What? I can't believe you even still out here, Moe. You know Jenny got'chu on curfew," Nut clowned again.

"Wateva, nigga, I'm out'chere!" said Moe.

"Maan, I got'chu, Nut. You ain't gotta spend shit," Lee offered.

Nut rubbed his beard in a pensive state.

"I call that," Nut agreed.

58

"A'ight, shid, it's a lil' after ten. Let's catch sounds, and grab a fit before he closes," Lee suggested.

"You payin' for my shit?" asked Nut.

"I told ja, I got'cha, my nigga. Let's slide."

"Yo' cheap ass," Ricardo added, as everybody hopped in Lee's BMW X6. As soon as Lee started the whip, the sounds of Rod Wave's "Dark Clouds" blared from the set of JL Audios.

Lord I'm just a nigga tryna win / Lord I'm just a nigga so I sin / We spin his block, we spin his block / Then spin again, mmh / He gotta pay for what he did—

"Maan, that nigga Rod Wave be slidin'!" Lee stated, turning the volume down.

"He a'ight. That nigga cry too much for me," Ricardo voiced while Moe fiddled with his phone.

"He just got album of the year, nigga, numbers don't lie," Lee retorted laconically, turning off of Kent Kerns St. into a plaza where *Sound Clothing* store was located.

"Aye, shhhh! Turn the music off," Nut exclaimed, brimming with excitement.

"Fuck wrong wit'chu?" questioned Ricardo.

"See them niggaz going in the store?"

"What about'em?" asked Lee

"What up, Nut?" said Moe

"That's them D.C. niggaz that robbed me," Nut announced warily.

"What'chu wanna do?" Moe asked, pulling a Glock .40.

"Maan, I'on wanna use no pistol. And we can't use this truck. Run me back to Smitty's right quick. I got two sticks in a baser rental on the side of Smitty's. Hurry up, nigga!" yelled Nut. Lee got on the gas and was back at Smitty's in two minutes. Four minutes later, Nut, Moe, and Ricardo were sitting in the parking lot of *Sound Clothing*. With no time to grab ski masks, they all tied shirts around their faces. Moments later, the door to *Sound Clothing* opened.

"Yo' slim, you seen how baby was checking for me in there?" Ox asked Worm.

"You got to be crazy, Ox! Shorty was all over me, slim," Worm replied, not paying attention to what was in front of him. He bumped into a beautiful Trinidadian woman who was pushing her baby in a stroller.

"Pardon me, ma," Worm apologized.

"It's okay—"

Ka Ka Ka Ka Ka Ka Ka! Ka Ka Ka Ka Ka Ka!

"Uh huh!" Nut exclaimed, feeling hyped all the way.

Ka Ka Ka Ka Ka Ka Ka! Ka Ka Ka Ka Ka Ka Ka!
All the windows in *Sound Store* shattered and fell to the ground along with Ox and Worm. Nut and Moe trotted back to the car, while Ricardo walked up on Ox and Worm, who were twisted on the pavement with chunks of flesh missing from their bodies. The 76.2 rounds made it look like *Jaws* had took a bite out of Ox's and Worm's flesh. Ricardo also saw the beautiful woman and her baby slaughtered a few feet away.

"You niggaz got down south fucked up. Na look at'cha. City of no Pity, stupid niggaz." *Boc! Boc!* After putting a hole in each of their heads, Ricardo made his way back to the whip.

Nut turned a few corners, met up with Lee who was waiting, switched cars, and slipped away unnoticed.

Chapter Twelve

We Got a Problem

"Da - Da! Da - Da!" Assata yelled repeatedly as she pulled on Khafre's dredz and drooled on his apparel.

"Damn, baby girl, you just gone drool on daddy?" Khafre said, kissing his daughter on the cheek.

"Da - Da! Da - Da!"

"Khafre, we need to talk," Quen insisted with a trace of impatience. Khafre gave her an evaluative look.

"Wassup? Sit down, and talk to me," Khafre said, his curiosity piqued, Quen had a seat next to him and Assata. She then looked him in his eyes and exhaled cynically.

"I'm tired of sittin' around this house."

"Okay. So what'chu got in mind?"

"I wanna start back doing body contouring and physical therapy. I haven't been productive lately."

"You just had a whole baby," countered Khafre.

"I know but I wanna get back in the groove of things." Khafre's phone rang.

"Here, get Assata." He handed Quen the baby. "We'll discuss this later. Yeah, wassup?" Khafre answered his phone.

"We gotta problem," informed Ketta.

"I'm in ya chest in a few minutes."

"Okay," Ketta said.

Khafre hung the phone up.

"I gotta handle some shit. Watch Assata and the boys." Without waiting on a reply, Khafre got up and headed out.

***

It was a beautiful but hot summer day. When Khafre rounded the corner of 23rd, Tay was dipped in Balmain from head to toe, serving cars that were lined up on the side of the road. Poised in an all-black fitted Dior t-shirt, sweats and a beanie, Khafre waited patiently until Tay was done.

"What dey do, lil' homie?" Khafre inquired in a molly tone.

"You already know! I know you see I got this bitch swagin' out'chere," Tay replied, smirking mischievously.

"Yeah, I peeped that. I peeped you went against the coalition too."

"Maan, fuck all that peace treaty shit! Them niggaz been the ops, they gone stay the ops! It's forever up there wit' me! Certified Crayz E status! Red Rum, nigga!" Tay stated, boldly throwing up Deuce Trey, influencing two of his young hittaz to approach the scene from under the tree where they were posted. Khafre smiled unbothered.

"I hear you and I see you lil' nigga. Unfortunately, yo' conduct has become a problem. If you don't kill a problem at its roots, the solution is only temporary," Khafre philosophized.

"Fuck is you sayin', old head?" Tay asked threateningly, snatching out his pistol.

"It's gone be a cold summer, lil' homie," Khafre retorted, assuredly turning his back on Tay and walking off.

Boc! Nose, who was one of Tay's hittaz, drilled a neat red hole in the side of Tay's head, dropping him dead. Nard, also one of Tay's hittaz planted two hot ones in Tay's chest. Tay fell asleep in a puddle of blood on the sidewalk while his killers fled the scene. Tay had killed a youngin' from the projects, breaking the peace treaty. Khafre put two bricks on Tay's head, and his own lil' homies took the offer.

Chapter Thirteen

Eat!

It was a dying afternoon, and the sun was quite low in its setting, creating an abstract design across the sky. Khafre had Ketta bent over in her unmarked car, while he stood on the outside and punished her pussy from the back.

"Ooww, shit! Sss—fffuck! I love this dick! Sss! Yes! Fffuck me, nigga!" Ketta moaned while looking back at Khafre. Khafre applied more pressure, causing Ketta to crawl forward.

"Um-uh! Come here!" Khafre stated, grabbing her by the waist and pulling her towards him.

"Yes, daddy! Take this pussy!" Ketta cried, gripping the interior in the back seat.

"N'all, bitch, take this dick!" Khafre said through clenched teeth.

"Ssss—aww—I'ma—take—it—daddy!" She growled, cumming for the second time. Khafre grabbed both of her velvet-soft ass cheeks and spread them wide as he could. He then stood on his toes, put a dip in his back and began to stroke her wet pussy hard and steady.

"Sss—ffuck yeah! Push dem fuckin' cheeks back! Sss—aaaahh!" Ketta yelled and began to shake uncontrollably as she came.

"I'm on my way!" Khafre growled, cuming right behind her.

"Shit!" stated, Khafre when his phone rang. He snatched out of Ketta, reached in his back pocket and answered his phone.

"Yeah, what up?" Ketta turned around and began to clean Khafre's dick with her mouth.

"I'm back in town, I need to see you," Nut pronounced.

"Fffuck!"

"What happen?" questioned Nut.

"Sshit! Nothin' bra. Just meet me at the Brown store in twenty minutes," Khafre said with his left hand in Ketta's hair.

"A'ight, I'll be there. I'm already around the corner," exclaimed Nut.

"Already!" *Click!* Khafre hung the phone up.

***

By the time Khafre pulled into the Brown store, the sun had disappeared completely. The night was cool and the store's traffic was mild. Khafre spotted Nut and an unfamiliar face sitting in a rental car on the side of the store. He approached them.

"What up, nigga?" asked Khafre

"Wassup, mane?" Nut retorted, getting out of the car and dapping Khafre up.

"Who you got wit'cha?" asked Khafre, consumed with curiosity.

"Oh, that's my peoples. He straight," Nut assured.

"Yeah, a'ight. So, what the play is? You going back up there to hustle without takin' care of that problem?"

"Come on, mane. You know I'on mind bustin' a nigga head. That shit, taken care of," Nut stated, grinning mischievously.

"That's wassup. So, how many you need?"

"Just give me two."

"Wea that paper at?" Nut motioned for his people to hand him the bag.

"Money on deck, mane," asserted Nut, handing Khafre a paper bag. Khafre looked in the car, then back at Nut.

"You sho', fool straight?" questioned Khafre, lowering the lid of one eye significantly.

"I told you that's my people. He solid, man. I wouldn't put'chu in no type of situation to lose." Khafre noted the whole supplicant in Nut's manner.

"Yeah, me neither," said Khafre. "Give me a minute. I gotta run upstairs," exclaimed Khafre, spinning off and heading upstairs to his apartment. Khafre entered his apartment, locked the door behind him and headed to his bedroom. He placed the bag on his bed, then grabbed a half of blunt that was in an ashtray on the nightstand and put flame to it. He inhaled deeply, held it for a brief moment, then exhaled slowly as he stood in a pensive state.

"Why the fuck would Nut bring a nigga I'on know to handle bidness?' Khafre thought out loud. "You trippin', homie," Khafre muttered, reaching for the bag, blunt pinched between his lips. He then dumped the money on the bed. After eye balling the money, he hit the blunt, then pulled out his phone to make a call.

"Wassup wit' it?" asked the caller.

"Eat!"

***

"Maan, wassup wit'cha man's?" Lil' Haiti said.

"He straight, trust me," Nut assured.

"Man, dude was lookin' like I'm the police, or some shit."

Nut chuckled at Lil' Haiti's comment.

"What's so funny, bra?"

"Well, you did tell on that hoe when them crackaz jammed you. You kinda is the police," clowned Nut.

"Maan, fuck you!"

"I'm just sayin'."

"Man, wassup wit'cha homie? He taken too long," whined Lil' Haiti.

"Chill, he comin'. Just relax." Nut grabbed his whopper from Burger King and unwrapped it. "Damn, they put cheese on my burger." Nut peeled the cheese off and offered it to Lil' Haiti.

"You want this cheese?"

"Oh, you a comedian na?"

"What'chu talkin' 'bout?" Nut asked, confused.

"You tryin' to give me cheese? You tryin' to say, I'ma rat?"

Nut laughed in Haiti's face.

"I wasn't even thinkin' 'bout it like that, but that shit is funny." He continued to laugh.

"Maan, I ain't fuckin' wit'chu after this. This it!"

"Man, calm down. You still my nigga. A lot of niggaz out here got police ass homeboys, shid, at least you ain't gay." Nut laughed again. Nut's laughter was cut short when he saw two figures appear in front of his car in all-black.

"Oh shii—." Nut tried to leap into the back seat.

Ka Ka Ka Ka Ka Ka Ka—Ka Ka Ka Ka Ka Ka Ka!
Ka Ka Ka Ka Ka Ka Ka—Ka Ka Ka Ka Ka Ka Ka!

The two assailants peppered the vehicle with 76.2 rounds then took off. When Khafre made his way downstairs and looked into the car, half of Nut's body was in the back seat and half still in the front. Lil' Haiti had so many holes in him, that his likeness was that of a creature from a sci-fi film.

"Treason means death, stupid nigga," Khafre stated with no empathy. He walked off, got in his vehicle and pulled away. Nut had given Khafre counterfeit bills; he had to die. Before meeting Nut at the Brown store, Khafre had called T-Byrd from the projects and Lloyd from 113th St. Even though they hated each other, they put their differences to the side for a chance to kill Nut, who had been a problem for them many years now. They had just proved their loyalty to the coalition. Khafre gave them a brick apiece.

Chapter Fourteen

Massacre

"You know you live right down the street from your grandmother, Patty, don't chu?" Shantel inquired as she sat in the back seat of Khafre's Rover and ate a seafood platter from Patty's.

"Yeah, I heard," Khafre replied with an air of dismissal.

"So, why haven't you gone to see her then?" Khafre glanced in the rear view mirror, and gave his mother a knowing look.

"You know why. Stop playin' crazy." It took Shantel a moment to understand what Khafre meant.

"Oh, I forgot about that," Shantel stated, remembering that Khafre had killed Patty's daughter and two grandkids.

"Forgot about what?" Quen asked from the front seat.

"It ain't nothin' to talk about. Don't worry 'bout it," said Khafre.

"Well, I wanna meet your grandmother."

"You gone have to do that shit on ya own time," he replied coldly. Quen was confused at Khafre's remark.

"Mama, clear yo' schedule for next week."

"For what?"

"I booked you a cruise for Jamaica. You leave next week."

"For real?"

"Yeah, you need a break, mama. Go, enjoy ya self."

"Thank you so much, baby," Shantel said, hugging Khafre's neck from the back seat.

"Come on na, you gettin' crab juice all on a nigga clothes and shit," Khafre complained, turning right off of

Okeechobee road into a plaza. Quen sat in silence while gazing at Khafre with malice in her heart.

"Fuck is yo' problem?" he asked.

"So you don't think I need a vacation?" asked Quen.

"You ain't got time to waste on no vacation."

"How you figure that?" countered Quen briskly.

"Kuz you gotta stay in the city to run this," Khafre retorted, pointing at a building that read "Physical Therapy and Body Contouring by Quen." Quen looked up and gasped.

"Oh my God! Baby, what did you do?" Quen stepped out of the truck to get a better look.

"Watch the kids, mama. Let me show her inside."

"I got'em," Shantel assured. Khafre got out of the truck, when Quen rushed him and hugged his neck.

"Thank you so much, baby!"

"Oh now it's *thank you*? You were just lookin' like you wanted to cut me."

"I'm sorry, baby."

"Yeah, whateva. Go check it out," he insisted, handing her the keys to the building. Quen kissed Khafre, grabbed the keys and headed inside. Khafre was following behind her when his phone rang.

"Talk to me!" he answered.

"Everythang in motion," T-Byrd stated.

"Give me twenty minutes," replied Khafre.

"Say none," *Click!*

***

It was an attractive sunny day outside on 14th Street, but the air was thick with ambivalence behind Lil' Haiti and Nut's death. There was plenty of weed, x-pills, and liquor but nothing could assuage the pain of losing two loved Haitians.

"Man, I heard it was them niggas from the projects," said David.

"N'all, they sayin' them niggaz from the plaza did it," Lee added.

"Maan, fuck it! Anybody who ain't Haitian gettin' flipped!" David announced.

"Long live Nut!" yelled a Haitian mami wearing a catsuit that displayed Nut's face on it.

"Go sit'cha drunk ass down! We talkin' over here!" said Lee, when four Tahoe's pulled up with Haitian flags tied on the trucks antennas playing Lil' Haiti's favorite song by Yhung T.O.

I've been runnin' up a check / Slidin', gang members hopping out with TEC's / Niggas can't afford this price on my neck / Glock-19 when I'm slidin' through the 'jects / I lost my lil' brother to these streets / So it ain't a question why I gotta keep the heat / A lot of niggas mad, I spent a dub in a week / I be seeing death when I close my eyes to sleep

All driver doors of the Tahoes opened simultaneously with men stepping out of trucks and popping out of the sunroofs. They all had Haitian flags tied around their mouths and AK's in their hands. All at once 76.2 rounds began flipping out of the rifles and knocking chunks from everybody in sight. Each rifle had one-hundred-round drums attached to them. When every round was spent there wasn't a body in sight with breath in it. Everybody on 14th Street was dead. The shooters hopped back in the trucks and pulled away. Five minutes later, they all pulled into a ducked off spot on South 113th Street that was owned by Ketta. Once inside, Khafre and other members of the coalition removed the Haitian flags from around their faces.

70

"Listen up!" Khafre demanded, grabbing everybody's attention.

"Somebody tried to take food from our plates, and the plates of our loved ones. If you know me by now, then you know that's a no-no! Disobedience simply means death! Treason means death! Cowardice means death!"

"Talk dhat shit my, nigga!" yelled Lloyd, hyped by Khafre's words. Khafre raised his hand as if to silence Lloyd so he could continue.

"Once again you've put aside your differences for the betterment of the coalition. We are the coalition!" Khafre yelled, pistol in the air.

"The coalition!" everybody yelled in unison, rifles in the air. Khafre knew that there would be problems behind Lil' Haiti's and Nut's deaths, so he eliminated all threats.

Chapter Fifteen

Motherfuka!

Seven Years Later—

Everybody that was a part of the coalition was either dead or in jail.

Instead of continuing to do business with gang members, Khafre just kept a few old heads in his pocket that only copped three bricks a month. He had more than enough money to go legit, but it was something about the game that made him feel alive.

"Hassan, tell me about character," Khafre insisted while rolling a joint at the kitchen table.

"Character matters more than reputation," Hassan answered.

"And why is that?"

"Because character reflects who you are on the inside, reputation is tied to what others think about you. Reputation develops from character."

"That's correct." Khafre handed Hassan five-hundred dollars, then sparked his blunt.

"Husain, tell me about reality." Husain exhaled irritably before answering.

"Reality is seeing things for what they are, not how or what you want them to be."

"A'ight, what else?" Khafre asked, blowing smoke from his nose.

"Things and people are not what we wish them to be or what they seem to be, they are what they are."

"That's correct. Why you act like you had a problem answering the question? You don't want the money?" questioned Khafre, handing Husain the money.

"I still have the money you been giving me every day. I wanna go outside," whined Husain.

"I'ma let'chu go in a minute. Assata, tell me about silence."

"Okay, daddy!" Assata stated excitedly. "Silence speaks volumes. Those who are not talking can listen."

"Okay, what else, baby girl?"

"Um—listening opens the way of learning."

"What is learning?

"Learning is knowledge, knowledge is power. Without power everything is an illusion."

"That's my baby girl. Here you go." Khafre handed her the money.

"Thank you, daddy."

"Anything for you, baby girl. Husain, you can go outside now. Hassan, you too."

"Yeess!" yelled Husain as he removed himself from the table and headed outside.

"I'm good, pop. I'ma just go play the game," Hassan asserted, then headed to his room.

"What about'chu, Assata?"

"I'ma go play the game with Hassan, daddy." Assata kissed her father on the cheek then headed to Hassan's room.

***

Khafre had called Quen's phone for the third time, only to be sent to the voicemail again.

"I know, this bitch see me callin'," Khafre muttered when Husain ran back inside crying hysterically.

"Boy, what the hell, wrong wit'chu?" Husain ignored his father and reached under the sofa cushion. He grabbed a wet mud Glock 30, that he'd seen Khafre place under the sofa cushion many times and ran back outside.

"Husain!" Khafre yelled, getting up to follow his son. When he made it outside, he saw Husain running towards a group of teens with the pistol hidden behind his back. He started to call Husain, in an attempt to stop him, but saw that he was too far gone. Husain had blood in his eyes.

"Give me back my money!" Husain yelled, revealing the pistol and pointing it at the crowd. He then turned his head, closed his eyes and fired.

Boc!

"Aaah!"

Boc!

"Uuuhhh!"

Boc!

"Hhuuh!"

Boc! Boc! Boc! Boc! Boc! Boc! Boc! Boc! Boc! Boc!

Husain let off all thirteen shots and kept squeezing after the clip was empty. He had zoned out until he heard Khafre's voice. Husain opened his eyes and saw three of the teens laid out on the pavement. The rest could be seen running for their lives. Husain turned and ran back to his father crying.

"Poppa, I'm going to jail!" Husain cried, flaring his arms about. Khafre took the gun from Husain.

"Listen, relax! I ain't gone let'chu go to jail. Stop that crying and go get in the shower."

"Daddy, what happened?" Assata asked, voice soft as a purring leopard.

"Go back in the room, baby girl. I'll be in there in a minute." Assata turned away with no argument and headed to her room.

"What happened, pop?" asked Hassan.

"Yo' brother just got his first taste of being a man."

"What'chu mean, pop?"

"Some boys tried to take his money. He shot some folk, probably killed some. If you would have been out there wit'em, this wouldn't have happened. From now on, y'all stay together. No matter what! You hear me?"

"Yes, popa," Hassan said with his head down feeling as if he'd let his father down.

"Hold ya head up, boy. Don't ever hold your head down for nothin! Head up, ten toez down! You hear me?"

"Yes, popa."

"What I tell you 'bout being soft?"

"Softness is weakness, comprise is disastrous, and tolerance is fatal," Hassan answered briskly.

"A'ight, go check on ya brother."

"Yes, popa," replied Hassan, walking off. Moments later a crowd could be heard gathering out front. Khafre took the pistol, grabbed a brown bag from the kitchen cabinet, and headed outside.

"Motherfuka! Yo' son shot three of my nephews!" yelled Ms. Ann.

Husain had shot Pookie in the leg, Bee Bop in the thigh, and P-Brian in the ass. All three were brothers from the projects.

"Calm down, miss lady. Now are they still alive?" asked Khafre.

"Yeah, they alive! But'cho son goin' to jail!"

"Okay, where is the mother?" Khafre questioned, clutching the pistol in case one of the men who were with the mob got too aggressive.

"They mama dead, I take care of them!" Ms. Ann exclaimed.

"Here." Khafre handed her a bag with fifteen grand in it.

"I'm sure, that should make this lil' problem go away." Ms. Ann looked in the bag and got wide eyes.

"Come on, y'all! Let's go! Sorry to bother you, Mister," stated Ms. Ann, walking away. Khafre chuckled,

Chapter Sixteen

Look at This Shit

"Line the target up like I told you, exhale and squeeze," Khafre explained to Husain. After watching Husain close his eyes while shooting, he made it his business to make him a marksman. Khafre knew first-hand that being timorous behind a gun could be fatal. He'd taken Kurt's life for this same mistake.

"I am!" whined Husain.

"Shut up and listen. Keep ya eyes open! And hold that shit wit' two hands!

This ain't no gangsta movie! This real life! If them boys you shot had a gun, they coulda killed you! Don't never in yo life again close yo' eyes, and turn yo' head when you tryin' to take a life. If you pull a gun, you look your victim in the eyes and shoot to kill! You hear me?"

"Yes, sir," Husain said.

"A'ight then, get off!" Khafre ordered.

Boc! Boc! Boc! Khafre had posters taped to a tree with cop faces on them deep in some woods in Okeechobee.

"That's what the fuck I'm talkin' bout!" Husain had hit his target in the eye, the nose, and in the right side of the head. Husain smiled diabolically.

"A'ight, Hassan. Let that shit go!" Khafre demanded. Hassan had watched and listened to the instructions his father had given Husain, so his accuracy was next to perfection.

Boc! Boc! Boc! Boc! All Hassan's shots were planted in the middle of the targets head.

"Boy! You're a natural born sniper! Good fuckin' shot!"

"Thanks, pop," Hassan replied. Husain patted Hassan on the back.

"Good shot, bra!" Husain admitted. Hassan thanked him.

"Daddy, can I try?" Assata smiled excitedly.

"Okay, let me get'chu a smaller one," said Khafre, reaching for a .25 FN pocket rocket. He then handed it to Assata. Assata shook her head, by way of saying: *No*.

"I don't want that one," she said with a look of disgust.

"I wanna shoot that one." Assata pointed at a FN .40.

"That's too big, baby," Khafre cautioned.

"I can shoot it, daddy," she said pleadingly.

"Okay, baby, here." Khafre placed it in her hands and stood behind her in an attempt to assist her.

"I got it, daddy," she exclaimed, slightly irritated.

"Okay, princess. Go ahead." Khafre stepped back. Assata held the pistol tight with both hands. It moved slightly up and down in her attempt to keep a steady aim, but when she lined the target up, exhaled and squeezed, she'd planted one in the midsection of the target.

"Good shot, baby!"

Boc! Boc! Boc! Assata let off three more shots, each one finding a mark further up the body. She planted one in the chest, neck, and chin.

"Damn, good shot!" Khafre cheered, surprised at what he was seeing.

"I told you I could do it," Assata stated arrogantly. Khafre's phone beeped. He pulled it out and saw that his ADT alarm system had alerted him that there was motion in the building that he'd bought for Quen.

"Look at this shit, here," he muttered, smirking.

"What daddy?" asked Assata.

"Nothin', baby. Let me see that shot again."

***

Quen was in the process of wrapping things up with a client, when another potential client entered her place of business.

"I'll be right with you, ma'am. Just give me a moment. I have plenty of refreshments, just help yourself. The blonde looked over the refreshments, but touched nothing. She took a seat and waited to be seen.

"Okay, so you've been scheduled for next month on the 9th at twelve-thirty—I'll see you then," Quen stated.

"Okay, thank you so much, Ms. Quen. I'll see you later," Antwon replied, projecting femininity.

"Okay, baby." Quen approached the blond-haired woman who wore Dior frames and stuck her handout. "Hi, welcome to *Body Contouring by Quen*. How can I help you, today, ummm?"

"Dynetta. My name is Dynetta."

"Nice to meet'chu, Dynetta. What can I do for you?"

"Umm, well, I noticed the sign when I was leaving Pizza Hut, and I was curious. What exactly is body contouring?"

"If you'd like, I can put'chu on the machine, and show you. First session is free," Quen said, confident in her sales pitch.

"Okay. We can do that," Dynetta stated, standing to her feet.

"Umm—If I may be honest, you really don't need body contouring. You already have a fat ass. Your body is perfect!" admitted Quen with lust in her eyes. Dynetta caught it.

"You into women?" Dynetta implored.

"I am bi. I love women," Quen asserted, smiling.

"Okay then, I guess it's a vibe. Let me ask you somethin' though."

78

"Yeah?"

"You get a lot of gay dudes in here?"

"Oh yeah, girl. They are my main customers, and they tip healthy too."

"Get that paper, girl. I'm feelin' that. So what I gotta do?"

"You are gonna have to take your pants and panties off."

"I don't wear panties, girl. Makes me feel restricted."

"That's even better," Quen proclaimed, excited to see this yellow beauty naked.

"That's a plan, but I'm not laying on that, until you sanitize it. I'm not homophobic, but bitch, monkey pox is real!" Dynetta clowned.

'You crazy, girl! You know I'ma sanitize before we get started. Give me a second." Quen grabbed her sanitizer and began cleaning the peach-colored leather bed.

"Um just saying you can never be too careful."

Boc! Dynetta planted one in the back of Quen's head and left the building. Once she was back in the stolen Land Rover, Ketta removed the blond wig and pulled off. Dynetta was really Ketta. Khafre had ordered Quen's death after his ADT alarm system showed her having sex with one of the old heads he did business with by the name of Metro. Khafre would have spared her life if she would have fucked him respectfully. But she fucked him in a place of business that he'd bought for her. She had to go.

Chapter Seventeen

I Promise

Khafre was cleared after proving to homicide detectives that he was at the mall with his kids. He conjured up a few tears to appear mournful, but knew he would be exonerated. Ketta was one of the detectives. Khafre's only dilemma was breaking the news to Assata.

"Peter, I'll meet'chu to the car. I need to speak with Mr. Moss for a moment," Ketta told the rookie detective.

"Yes, ma'am." Peter turned and walked away. When Ketta heard the front door close, she approached Khafre, wrapped her arms around him and kissed him deeply.

"See, baby. I told you I got'chu," exclaimed Ketta, chuckling cynically.

"What I owe you?"

"Some dick." She rubbed her pussy against Khafre's dick. Khafre gripped her ass cheeks then kissed her on the neck.

"Look, I'ma catch you later. I gotta go in here and tell my showty's wassup." Assata, who was peeking around the wall of the hallway, turned quickly and headed to Hassan's room.

"Okay, daddy." Ketta kissed Khafre and left. After locking the front door, Khafre headed to Hassan's room. When he entered, all three of his kids were piled in Hassan's HiCan bed. A modern-day canopy with a built-in HD projector, and 70-inch home theater screen. It ran Khafre a cool one-hundred thousand, and all three of his kids had one.

"Y'all pause that game, I need to talk to y'all for a minute." Hassan paused the game, then Husain sucked his teeth. Khafre gave Husain a knowing look that prompted him to lighten his face expression.

"Wassup, pop?" asked Hassan. Khafre exhaled before speaking.

"Quen is gone."

"Mommy?" Assata questioned.

"Yea, baby."

"Gone where?" Hassan asked.

"Somebody came in her shop and shot her. She dead."

"Nooo!" cried Assata. She got off the bed and approached her father. Khafre squatted to embrace her. Hassan held his head down and thought about his mother. The memory of his mother stretched out on the floor in a puddle of blood pervaded his mind, causing a single tear to fall down his right eye. Husain sat in silence processing everything. Even though Quen wasn't his mother, he'd grown to love her.

"It's gone be okay, baby," Khafre whispered in Assata's ear.

"Nooo! No, it's not!" Assata yelled, pushing Khafre off of her.

"Baby girl."

"No! Why didn't you protect her?" Assata yelled, her fist clenched by her side.

"There was nothin' I could do, baby," Khafre said, reaching out to grab Assata, who pushed his hands away aggressively.

"Lies! You said that grandpa told you to protect what you love! You didn't protect mommy, because you didn't love her!" Assata screamed, sending a chill throughout Khafre's body. Deep down he knew she was right. Assata peppered Khafre's face with a combination, forcing him to cover his face.

"It's gone be okay, baby," he assured. When Assata grew tired from punching Khafre's arms, she hugged him and cried her heart out. Khafre held her tight, feeling somewhat guilty.

"I'm sorry, baby girl. Daddy loves you. Everything gone be a'ight. I promise."

***

"Pops."

"Wassup?"

"How come we don't have any cousins, aunties, or uncles?" Hassan asked out of the blue. Khafre glanced at him, caught off guard by the question.

"Yeah, pops," Hussain added.

"Yeah, daddy, how come?" Assata chimed in.

"Y'all did have cousins, aunties, and uncles. They all died before y'all was born," stated Khafre.

"But why?" questioned Assata.

"Because—baby—they were all killaz. Y'all come from a family of killaz, and sometimes killaz get killed for the things they did."

"So, the person who killed mommy is gonna pay, right?" Assata said.

"Of course, baby. Hassan go in the store."

"Yes, sir," Hassan said, getting out of the car to head inside of the Brown store. Once inside the Brown store, Hassan headed straight for the chip rack and grabbed a big bag of *Lay's* potato chips. He then headed to the counter to pay for them.

"Excuse me, Mister," Hassan said to a man who was standing in front of him scratching a scratch off ticket.

"Wassup, lil' man. You tryin' to pay for ya chips, huh?"

"Yes, sir," replied Hassan, attempting to hand Wolly the money.

"Don't worry about it. I'll pay for them," exclaimed the man with the scratch offs.

"Thank you, Mister." Hassan opened the chips, ate a few then headed back outside. "That's a nice old man," Hassan muttered to himself. Moments later the Scratch Off man exited the store, still scratching tickets.

"That was a nice thing you did, Mister."

"Awl, it's nothin', lil' man," said the Scratch Off man.

"Want some?" Hassan offered, reaching into the chip bag.

"I'm Koo—" *Boc!* Hassan had pulled a compact micro Hellcat from the chip bag, and planted one in Mr. Scratch Off's head. The last thing Hassan heard before jumping in the car with Khafre was the sound of the quarter hitting the pavement, that Mr. Scratch Off used for his tickets. Once in the car, Khafre pulled off and disappeared. Husain had a big smile plastered on his face. Watching someone get their head bust always brought joy to Husain.

"You did good, that was perfect," Khafre stated.

"Yeah, Hassan, you got'em good," added Assata.

"Thanks." Hassan replied in a molly tone. Khafre studied his face to try to determine how Hassan was feeling after his first kill, but couldn't pinpoint it.

"How you feel?"

"I'm cool, pops. Can we get Popeyes?" Hassan asked. *Oh, yeah, I gotta natural born killa*, Khafre thought to himself.

"Yeah, we can do that, after we switch cars," Khafre replied.

The man that Hassan had just killed was Metro. Metro was someone who Khafre conducted business with. He was also the man that Quen was having sex with on camera.

"So why did Mr. Metro have to die?" questioned Khafre.

"Because he disrespected the family," Hassan answered.

"How do we feel about family?"

"Family first!" exclaimed Husain.

"All the time," Khafre added.

"Daddy, I wanna catch one next," Assata announced.

"Catch what, baby?"

"A body," she stated assuredly. Khafre glanced in the rearview mirror at Assata, astounded.

"What'chu know 'bout, catchin' a body?"

"GTA." Khafre chuckled at her response.

"This is real life, baby girl, not a video game."

"I know, but I can do it, daddy," Assata pleaded.

"Not right now, baby. But you'll get'cha chance."

"Promise?"

"Yeah, baby, I promise."

Chapter Eighteen

The City is Ours

Two Years Later—

Hassan and Husain hopped out of a stolen 2022 Lotus Emira, and headed inside a gate that surrounded a football field to attend a Pop Warner's game on 13th Street. In the past two years Hassan and Husain had been in multiple shoot outs. They were always dripping in designer and bust down jewelry, so they were always targets for the unfortunate. Being on 13th Street was risky, but they refused to miss out on the half-naked women that attended. Now fifteen years old, with reputations that preceded them, they felt like "gods amongst men".

"Heeyy, Husain," said a Spanish beauty named Tasha. Husain and Tasha had been vibing on *Facebook*, and seeing each other in a teen club dubbed "Molly World". She had a sister named Lee Lee, who was also Latina and black. Husain had made it his bidness to hook Hassan up with her.

"Wassup wit'it?" Husain replied.

"Why you ain't call me back last night?" Tasha asked, her excitement evident.

"I got caught up," Husain replied arrogantly.

"Umm-humm. I guess," Tasha fired back, smiling seductively while running her hand through her natural, long, sandy, wavy hair.

"Hi, Hassan." Lee Lee spoke, showing her perfect white teeth that contrasted sharply with her smooth, almost black, skin. Both young ladies were head turners, with celestial bodies that even had grown men gawking.

"Lee Lee, wassup, Queen? You lookin' like a whole vibe out'chere," Hassan admitted.

"What'chu gone do about it?" Lee Lee shot back briskly.

"Turn them lil' cheeks into dinner rolls." Lee Lee laughed, put her arms around Hassan and whispered in his ear.

"You know you still a virgin."

"N'all, yo' ass the one who fakin'. You know how I'm rockin'."

"We'll see after the game," Lee Lee challenged.

"I call that," Hassan said.

"Y'all want somethin' from the concession stand?" Husain offered.

"Yeah, get us some hot dogs," said Tasha. After getting the food, they found a spot on the bleachers, and tried to enjoy the game. The crowd went in a frenzy, when they saw Jacob break through the middle, break two tackles, and run the safety over before scoring his fourth touchdown for the Buccaneers.

"Damn! That Haitian fast as fuck!" Husain announced.

"That nigga ran like two niggaz over," Hassan added. Seconds later, Jacob trotted by the bleachers that Hassan and Husain were seated at and spoke his mind.

"Y'all loc ass niggaz on the wrong side of town, ana?" Jacob stated before running back to the huddle. Jacob was from 13th Street known as "O.T.G" (One Trey Gangstas). They were dubbed one of the most nefarious gangs in the city.

"Fuck you pussy ass, Haitian!" Husain yelled loud enough for everybody to hear.

"I think he mad because I stopped talkin' to him. We should just leave," Tasha suggested. Three members of 13th Street by the name of Bean, Larry, and Tim approached Hassan and Husain.

"You niggaz in violation! Get the fuck from 'round here, and take that shit back to the other side," exclaimed Larry.

"Pussy nigga, the city is ours! You fuck niggas just in the way! You niggaz ain't steppin' like us. Get'cha body count up, nigga!" Husain taunted, standing up and getting in their faces. Hassan stood with him.

"Y'all know 'bout 13th, nigga!" Tim stated.

"The niggaz before y'all was smokin' shit. Y'all niggaz is shit eaterz," Hassan retorted with an air of dismissal.

"My pops been putin' dirt on y'all niggaz big homiez," Husain added.

"Um, sayin' doe, Hassan. They say you shot me. Wassup, that was you?" asked Bean.

"Yeah, I shot'cha, bitch. That wasn't for you but'chu got in the way."

"So fuck ya! Wassup?" Hassan asked in a dangerously calm tone.

"You lucky we at this game. I'ma see you, doe," said Bean.

"Maaan, you can tell by the tone of my voice, I'on see that shit," Hassan said.

"Come on, y'all, let's just leave," Lee Lee advised, pulling Hassan by the hand.

"You niggaz know what time it is," Husain said, walking away with a wicked smile on his face. "It's gone be a cold summer!" he assured.

"Lee Lee and Tasha, keep them loc ass niggaz from over here," Tim asserted.

"Whatever, Tim!" Tasha said before leaving.

"So, wassup? What y'all finna get into?" questioned Husain.

"We gon' wit' y'all," Tasha stated.

"Y'all get in," Hassan said, starting the car.

"Which one of y'all got somebody who can get a room?" asked Hassan.

"My big sister can get it," Lee Lee replied. Hassan went in his pocket and handed Lee Lee two hundred-dollars.

"I'ma drop y'all off to yo' sister. Text me the hotel y'all at, and tell yo' sister she can keep the change," Hassan asserted.

"Okay," Lee Lee replied.

***

"Maan, that nigga Jacob was running them niggaz over! That nigga better than Barry Sanders," Tim boasted to Bean and Larry while making their way to Larry's father's truck.

"Fuck that game! What we gone do 'bout them loc's Hassan and Husain?" Larry said.

"Them niggaz ain't hard to find. They stay on Avenue S," Bean informed.

"Shid, I ain't gotta have my daddy truck back for another two hours. Wassup? Y'all wanna spin?" asked Larry.

"Ain't no question! Tasha and Lee Lee can get it too. Them hoez set trippin' for real," Tim added.

"What the fuck!" Larry muttered, stopping in front of his father's truck. A black Denali with five-percent tints was backed in next to his father's truck. The Denali was parked so close that it was impossible for Larry to get in the driver's seat of his father's Explorer.

"They outta pocket for real," said Bean, attempting to look inside the Denali, but the tint was too dark.

"We ain't got time to be waiting on the driver, I'ma just get in from the passenger side," Larry exclaimed. Larry

88

climbed in the driver's seat, Bean got in the passenger seat, and Tim hopped in the back seat.

"The pistols at my house. Slide by there, then we gone spin on them fuck niggaz," Tim announced.

"Bet," Larry replied, sticking the key in the ignition. The passenger window of the Denali began to roll down.

"Look, somebody in—" *Boc! Boc! Boc! Boc! Boc! Boc! Boc! Boc! Boc! Boc! Boc!* Tim's words were cut short by gunfire, people scattered.

"Stupid niggaz!" yelled Hassan who moved from the passenger seat to the driver's after putting multiple holes in Larry and Bean. Tim attempted to get as low as he could in the back seat, but to no avail. Husain rose from the bed of the Denali truck, with a M10 that had a box clip on it, holding two-hundred and fifty rounds. He sprayed the back of the Explorer with fifty rounds alone. Tim didn't stand a chance. He then sprayed the front of the truck with another 30 rounds for good measures. Husain laughed demonically before laying down in the bed of the truck. Hassan pulled off and slipped away under the moon.

Chapter Nineteen

Here We Go

"Ssssss! Haaasssan! Go slooow! You hurtin'
meeeeee!" Lee Lee cried, digging her nails' in Hassan's
flesh.

"My bad, I ain't tryin' to hurt'chu. I thought'chu
could stand this pressure," Hassan whispered in Lee Lee's
ear as he slowed his pace, and stroked her slow and deep.

"Haaaahh! Sss—ooowee—Yes! Just like that, baby,"
moaned Lee Lee as her pussy adjusted to the pressure.

"Shut up and take that dick!" Husain clowned while
getting his dick sucked by Tasha. She took Husain out of
her mouth to put her two cents in.

"You is really trippin'. That girl is a virgin, Husain,"
Tasha stated.

"You doing too much talkin', and not enough
suckin'! You know what?" Husain grabbed Tasha by her
hair, and shoved his entire dick in her throat.

"Aaahhggh!" Tasha gagged and threw up all over
Hussain's dick.

"Yeah!" Husain taunted then flipped Tasha on her
stomach before she could protest. He then put a pillow over
her head and entered her from behind.

"Ummmm! Sss! Yes! Fuck me!" Tasha growled, her
head still under the pillow.

"Damn!" moaned Husain, picking up his pace. After
catching her first nut, Tasha snatched the pillow from over
her head, looked back at Husain and began to throw her ass
back aggressively.

"Ol—ssshiit! Sss—Fffuck! That's it! Throw that
pussy back at this dick!" yelled Husain, loving how Tasha's
pussy felt.

"Uh-huh! Sss—yeah, nigga! Fuck you thought? Huh? Get it! This what'chu wanted, right? Huh? Tough ass nigga! Get this pussy!" Tasha taunted through clenched teeth, making her ass clap repetitiously.

"Oooooh—Ffffuck!" Husain cried, gripping and spreading her ass cheeks apart.

"Fight that shit, nigga!" Tasha motivated.

"Ssshit, um nutin' in this pussy!" growled Husain

"Sss—pussy skeatin' too, daddy! Ummmm—Yes!" Tasha bit her bottom lip, gripped the sheets and squirted all over Husain. She fell forward and clasped on the bed with Husain behind her.

"Get off me, nigga! Shit!" said Tasha. Husain rolled over and laid on his back, chasing his breath.

"Damn, that pussy was snatchin'," Husain admitted.

"Fuck me from the back?" Lee Lee asked Hassan.

"Turn over," Hassan replied. Lee Lee turned over.

"Damn! You bleeding," Hassan noted.

"Oh my God," Lee Lee cried.

"Don't trip. Come on, let's go take a shower." Hassan grabbed Lee Lee and led her to the shower.

"You ready for another round?" Husain asked.

"Nigga, is you ready?" Tasha shot back, grabbing Husain's dick. Before he could reply, his phone rang.

"Wassup, pop?" answered Husain.

"Where the fuck y'all at?" Khafre asked, concerned.

"Ducked off, why? Wassup?"

"I ain't seen y'all in three days."

"We good, pop," Husain assured.

"A'ight, but look here. Shit been echoing to me, right. So I gotta get' y'all down there to the investigation room."

"For what, pop?"

"Don't trip, lawyer on deck. Y'all get here, asap!" *Click!* Khafre hung the phone up.

"Damn. Look, Husain," Tasha showed him what Facebook news stated.

"Three teens slaughtered at Pop Warner's game. Brothers wanted for questioning."

"They got pictures of you and Hassan up. Did y'all do that?" questioned Tasha.

"Hell nawl! We been left that game. After dropping y'all off, we went to get clothes and food," lied Husain.

"People seen y'all get into it at the game." Tasha shook her head. "We just gone say y'all was with us," said Tasha.

"That's wassup. Aye, Hassan!" called Husain. Moments later, Husain and Tasha came from out of the bathroom.

"What's good, bra?" asked Hassan. Husain handed his brother the phone.

"Tsss—here we go," muttered Hassan.

***

After being interrogated by Ketta, Hassan and Husain were free to leave the police station. A few civilians mentioned the tension between the brothers and the three slain members from 13th Street gang, but no one was willing to testify that they'd actually seen the brothers commit the murders. Tasha and Lee Lee also vouched that the brothers were with them during the time the shooting occurred. Aside that, Khafre had retained Carren Tuff, one of the top lawyers in the Tri-County. The state didn't stand a chance at building a solid case. Tasha was now behind the wheel of her mother's Nissan Rogue, with no license. She'd stolen her mother's keys while she was sleeping to go pick Husain up.

"My moma gone kill me if she find out I took her car to come see you," Tasha said.

"Yo' moma know me?" Husain asked, his eyebrows raised.

"Yeah, I told her 'bout'chu," Tasha admitted.

"What exactly did you tell her?"

"I told her that I think I like you and that'chu a bad boy."

"And what she had to say 'bout that?"

"She wasn't too thrilled about it," Tasha said, making a left off of 13th Street and Avenue D.

"Well, I want'chu to set me an appointment for me to meet her."

"For what?" Tasha inquired.

"As good as that pussy is you totin' 'round, I got to meet the woman who made it. Ummm!" Husain clowned, grabbing his dick.

"Boy! Yeen got no kinda mind. You wanna fuck my mama?"

"Do I? Set that appointment up, yesterday." Tasha smiled and shook her head in disbelief.

"You just too much."

"Where you goin'?" Husain asked, his mood changing instantly.

"I'm just driving, why?" Tasha asked dumbfounded.

"You really gone just drive past the Blue Store, like I ain't in this car?" The Blue Store was one of the spots that 13th Street gang members posted at.

"This car got tints on it, we just driving by, calm down," Tasha replied.

"Yeah, a'ight," Husain exclaimed, snatching a Glock .357 from his Givenchy sweats.

"Husain, don't shoot outta my moma car!" Tasha warned. Husain remained silent as Tasha neared the Blue Store. When they were approximately 50 feet away from the store, Husain began to let down his window. Tasha made a quick right causing the Nissan's tires to screech.

The gangstaz in front of the store drew their weapons, ready to put holes in Tasha's mother's car.

"Wat the hell was that?" yelled Tasha, her heart racing.

"Act like you know what's goin' on. You know me and my brother got smoke wit' deez niggaz! Don't drive down 13th wit' me in the car, 'cause I'ma give it to them niggaz on every corner!" Husain said in a malevolent voice

"Me and my moma stay on 13th. Them niggaz know this car. At least have enough decency to catch them niggaz on yo' on time. Damn!" Tasha whined, stopping at a stop sign, on 12th Street in front of a graveyard.

"Yeen respecting my mind bringin' me 'round deez niggaz. Shid, my safety comes first," Husain countered.

"I'm just finna drop you off 'cause you trippin!" Husain looked up and seen a familiar face cross in front of the car. Jacob looked directly into the car, then stopped in front of it. Husain reached quickly, hopping out of the car, pistol in hand.

"Wassup, nigga?" asked Husain with murder on his mind.

"Husain, no!" screamed Tasha. When Jacob spotted the Glock in Husain's hand, he took off running. Husain pursued him with Tasha following behind them screaming for Husain to stop. Being a star running back, Jacob had a nice gap in between him and Husain. All of a sudden, Jacob stopped running and turned to face Husain.

"Fuck I'm running for? You ain't gone do shit, nigga," Jacob stated, sure of himself. *Boc! Boc! Boc!* Husain put three holes in Jacobs chest, dropping him. He stood over Jacob and was prepared to put a few more in his head, but Tasha pulled up and told him to get in the car. Husain left Jacob clutching on his chest, and hopped in the car with Tasha.

94

"Oh my gawd! You gone get me killed, or put in jail," Tasha exclaimed, her hands visibly shaking.

"Nobody ain't gone fuck wit'chu. That nigga should have kept it moving!" replied Husain with no empathy. Tasha shook her head as tears fell freely from her face.

Chapter Twenty

No Handle

"Yeah, it's all bad," Ketta stated somberly. They're holding him without bail, and they have a witness," she informed about Husain.

"Who the witness?" Khafre questioned.

"Some old guy by the name of Abraham. He lives on the corner of 12th and Avenue K. Also, they've charged him as an adult."

"A'ight. Don't worry 'bout the witness. Wassup wit' the girl who was driving the car?" Khafre asked, rubbing his chin.

"Tasha? She's out on an ankle monitor. Tasha solid, though, she ain't saying nothin'.'"

"That's wassup," Khafre said, pulling Ketta closer to him. "Listen, I appreciate'chu, ma." He gave her a forehead kiss.

"Anything for you, daddy," exclaimed Ketta, placing a tender kiss on Khafre's lips.

"You know, a couple of years ago, I prolly woulda killed you," he admitted. Ketta's face tightened with emotion.

"Why you say that?" Ketta asked, confused.

"I was on my black militant shit. Plus my father was killed by a dirty cop."

"Aahh! I'm not sure how to receive that. Should I consider myself lucky?" Ketta asked, using her hands for emphasis.

"Very!" said Khafre, grabbing Ketta's succulent ass cheeks and kissing her tenderly. Ketta reciprocated by putting her hand down Khafre's pants and massaging his growing shaft.

"Let me taste you, daddy," Ketta moaned seductively.

"Do you," replied Khafre.

"Daddy," Assata interrupted, standing in the hallway, peering into the living room. Ketta quickly removed her hand and took a step back.

"Yeah, baby, give me a minute," he told Assata. "Look, I'ma call you later, a'ight?"

"I'll be waiting," Ketta assured, then walked herself out. Assata then walked in and had a seat on the sofa next to Khafre.

"Wassup, baby girl?" Assata stared into her father's eyes for a few seconds. The air grew tense until she finally spoke.

"Do you love her?" Assata asked. Caught off guard by the question, Khafre shifted positions awkwardly before replying.

"No," he stated firmly.

"Do you still love mommy?"

Khafre exhaled then spoke his truth.

"You're the last and only woman I'll ever love," he answered with resignation.

"Promise?"

"I promise, baby girl." Assata moved closer and buried her head in her father's chest as a single tear cascaded down her right cheek.

"I love you, daddy."

"Love you too, baby."

***

It was a beauteous Friday summer evening. Civilians were rushing from work to get to their preferable vice, before going home to their loved ones. Hassan had on some Jordan 3 Retro and a Nike sweat suit as he dribbled a Spalding basketball through his legs down 12th Street.

"Wassup, nephew? You workin'?" a smoker asked Hassan as he passed him.

"N'all unk, I ain't doin' nothing'," Hassan replied and continued to dribble the ball down the street. When Hassan made it to Avenue K, it was an old head standing on the corner with his shirt off. He stood 6'2 and was chiseled like someone drew him.

"You pretty good wit' that ball, lil' homie. You play ball?" asked the old head. Hassan lost control of the ball, causing it to roll towards the old head.

"Oh, you ain't got no handle!" clowned the old head, bending down to pick up the ball. Hassan drew two baby pocket rocket .25 FN's from his sweats and punished Abraham, giving him all head shots.

"I just handled you though! Made a movie out'cha stupid ass! Police ass nigga!" Hassan boasted, then ran to the next corner, where he had a 250 Honda dirt bike laid against a tree. He hopped on it, headed to Taylor's Creek ditch bank and took it all the way home. Abraham was the witness in Hussain's case.

Chapter Twenty-One

Hunid Grand

After being charged as an adult, Husain was transferred from the juvenile detention center to St. Lucie's county jail. He'd only been there for three days and already he'd caught a battery on a detainee over a tablet. Now in the hole with added charges, Husain gazed at the walls, missing the streets until a guard banged on his cell door.

"Moss! You got a one-thirteen visit." Hussain climbed out of his bunk, and cuffed up. The C.O. ordered central to pop the cell.

"Mr. Moss, how you doing today?" Perkins asked.

"I'm facing a murder charge, how you think I'm feelin'?" Husain snapped.

"Hey, man, you put yourself in this situation. Handle that shit, man."

Perkins called for another door to be opened, then walked Husain towards one-thirteen.

"Tsss!" Husain complained, shaking his head.

"Your last name is Moss, huh? I've seen your grandfather and father come through here. You came from a vicious bloodline, and let me tell you. Your grandfather, and father walked through here with their heads high. Act like you know who you are, man," Perkins said before dropping Husain off to another guard over one-thirteen. Husain looked back at Perkins, surprised at his remark.

"Your visitor is already here. Go to *Room 7*," the overweight guard told Husain. He did as he was told and entered Room 7.

"Hey, Husain, I'm Detective Peter. How you doing, man?" Peter extended his hand for Husain to shake, but he declined. He looked upon the young European detective with disdain.

"Fuck you want, man?" questioned Husain, still standing.

"Trust me, you might wanna sit down," Peter advised.

"I think better on my feet."

"Alright then. It appears that the witness in your case was brutally murdered. You know anything about that?" asked Peter, interlocking his hands. Husain smiled before replying.

"How would I have knowledge of that? I'm in here. You got me recorded having knowledge of this? So, why you come here, fuckin' wit me, Detective?" Husain snapped.

"I can see how you find the deceased witness in your case amusing. But, you see, the footage we captured from the blue store camera's that's what I find amusing." Husain's face expression changed dramatically.

"Yeah, it shows you hopping out of Tasha's moma car, chasing Jacob with a pistol in your hand. However, it never captured Tasha behind the wheel. The witness had seen Tasha but he's now dead. The only person knows that Tasha was behind the wheel is you," Detective Peter stated, smiling knowingly.

"Who is Tasha?" Husain played stupid. Detective Peter arrogantly pretended to fix his tie as a jester of victory on the rise.

"Okay, here's how this is going to go. The prosecutor is going to show the camera's footage of you chasing Jacob with a gun, to an all-white jury and you will be convicted. You'll never see daylight again unless you tell me who the driver was. You give me Tasha, and I can guarantee you ten years. If not, the rest of your life's focus will be going half on a nacho, and watching episodes of Love and Hip-Hop." Husain rubbed his hand over his face, taking in everything he'd just heard.

"Pussy ass Kraka!"

***

Khafre was in Assata's room watching "Hidden Colors" with her on her HD projector, when his phone rang.

"Daddy, I'm hungry. Let's order from *Hungry Howies*," Assata suggested.

"Whatever you order, make sho' ain't no meat on that shit," Khafre said, grabbing his phone.

"I know this," Assata exclaimed, grabbing her phone to place an order.

"Yeah, wassup?" answered Khafre.

"Mr. Moss, hi, it's Carren Tuff," greeted Husain's lawyer.

"Carren, wassup?" Khafre asked, walking out of Assata's room and having a seat in the living room.

"Okay, so, listen. They have footage of Husain hopping out of a vehicle with something in his hands, chasing Jacob. Now, however, whatever's in Husain's hand, is not descriptive, and whatever happens to Jacob is not on camera. It doesn't show Husain committing the murder."

"So, we good then?"

"Let me finish. You see, I have an impeccable track record. I've never been defeated, I've never lost a case, and I never will. I don't take a case unless I'm positive I can win. Husain's case is a unique one. I know I can beat it, but he obviously doesn't believe in me," Carren said.

"What'chu mean?"

"Husain's turned state against Tasha for a plea of ten years.

"What!"

"I'll give you back half of the retainer. I'm off the case, Mr. Moss, I hate rats," Carren expressed disgust.

"You sho'?"

"Positive! Good day, Mr. Moss." *Click!* Carren hung the phone up. Before Khafre could process what he'd just heard, his doorbell rang. His cameras showed that it was Ketta. He headed to the front door and welcomed her in.

"Hey, baby," she greeted, hugging Khafre.

"Wassup? Listen, I need you to find somethin' out for me." Before Khafre could ask her anything, she handed him an envelope.

"Tasha's discovery!" she said. Khafre opened the envelope and began to read its contents. A single tear fell from the well of his eye as he read in black and white how his son turned coward. He'd pushed how important morality and integrity was into their heads over and over. To Khafre, telling was the ultimate betrayal, and Husain had told on a young woman who'd kept her mouth closed in an attempt to save him.

"I'm sorry, baby," Ketta sympathized, wiping the tears from Khafre's face.

"I gotta help him."

"How?" Ketta asked, confused.

"You know anybody who works in booking?"

"In the county jail?"

"Yeah."

"I know somebody who works in booking, why?"

"Pull up on neem. Tell'em to get on that computer, and release my son. I gotta hunid-grand." Ketta exhaled, knowing where this could lead.

"Okay, baby. I'ma see what I can do."

Chapter Twenty-Two

Moma!

Hassan played with his toy race car, while Husain laid sprawled out in the middle of the floor, asleep from exhaustion. He began to roll the car up Husain's leg, when he heard a commotion coming from the living room. He grabbed his toy race car and hobbled towards his room door, when he heard two muffled sounds followed by two thuds in tandem. Peeking out of his room, he saw the man who'd been playing with him and his brother standing over his mother and step mother, who appeared to both be sleeping. The nice man then hid something behind his back and came towards him.

"Wassup, lil' man?" the strange nice man asked Hassan. Hassan looked at the man, looked at his mother on the floor, then back at the strange man.

"You ready to come live wit' daddy?" Hassan waved to the man who in turned pulled what Hassan thought was a toy gun from behind his back and pointed it at him.

"Night, night." *Boc!*

"Aaahh! Moma!" Hassan awoke yelling and sweating profusely.

"Hassan. What's wrong? You okay?" Lee Lee asked, rubbing his sweaty back. Hassan could feel his heart beating rapidly in his chest. He wiped the sweat from his face with his right hand, then averted his attention to Lee Lee who had spent the night with him. She'd lied to her mother and told her she was sleeping over with her girlfriends.

"Yeah, I'm a'ight," Hassan responded as his heart rate gradually returned to its normal rate.

"You sho'?"

"Yeah, go back to sleep. I'm good," he assured. Jaded from intense sex, Lee Lee rolled over and quickly fell asleep. Hassan eased out of his HiCan canopy bed, reached under his pillow, grabbed a Glock .21 and slipped out of the room. He made his way down the spacious hallway that was embellished with African art, and slithered into his father's room. Khafre laid peacefully in a deep sleep, as Hassan tip-toed towards him with mixed emotions. When he reached the bed, a memory of his father carrying him out of a house while his mother laid stretched on the living room floor flashed through his mind. Did the man who was claiming to be his father kill his mother? Was he even his real father? Hassan's mind was bombarded with these thoughts, as he raised his pistol and aimed it at Khafre's right-side temple.

"Hassan." Hassan looked back and saw Assata attempting to wipe the sleepiness from her eyes. He quickly turned on his heels, placed the pistol behind his back and moved towards Assata.

"Come on," he whispered, leading her back to her room.

"What'chu was doing in daddy's room?" Assata whispered back.

"I was just checkin' on him," Hassan lied, tucking Assata (who was now eleven years old) back in bed.

"Okay," she whispered again and closed her eyes. Hassan gave her a forehead kiss, then headed back to his room. He laid next to Lee Lee and gazed at the ceiling in deep thought. Hassan couldn't prove if his father had killed his mother, but he knew wholeheartedly that the man who was claiming to be his father had taken initiative to instill morality and real life principles in him. He'd conjured his killer instinct, enabling him to survive in a cesspool of snakes. He'd loved and raised him and his brother effectually. Tears fell from Hassan's eye's at the thought of

104

killing his father. He tucked the pistol back under his pillow and just laid in suspended animation.

Chapter Twenty-Three

A Real Nigga Only Dies Once

"Bra, I got the chicken pattie from dinner. Let's put it in the goulash," Lil' Snoop suggested. Lil' Snoop was Husain's cellie from 23rd Street. He was in for a robbery beef.

"You know I'on eat that shit, fool. I'm vegan," Husain snapped.

"The fuck we suppose to eat? Chips and pickle?"

"You got commissary?"

"Nigga, you know my people don't fuck wit'me," Lil' Snoop retorted offensively.

"Well, shut the fuck up and put them beans in there, nigga," Husain said, washing his socks in the toilet.

"Bra, watch how you talk to me. I ain't one of them."

"Maan, what's next?" Husain asked, dropping his socks in the toilet and standing.

"Moss!" The unit guard spoke through the intercom.

"Yeah?"

"Pack your shit! You're outta here?"

"Where I'm goin'?"

"You going home! Be ready by the time I get there!"

"Shid, I'm ready na!" yelled Husain, his heart rate increasing from excitement.

"I'm on my way down!" *Click!*

"Damn, bra, you outta here," Lil' Snoop stated with mixed emotions.

Husain grabbed his bin and dumped all his commissary on the floor.

"You can have that shit!" Husain left his socks in the toilet and headed towards the door. Moments later, the guard came and opened the door.

"Moss!"

"Right here," Husain announced, showing the guard his wrist band. A few inmates were calling for Husain's attention, but he ignored them and left with the guard. When Husain reached booking, he dressed back out in his Givenchy sweatsuit and slipped on his Yeezy's with no sock.

"Moss, you wanna make a phone call?" asked the booking officer.

"N'all, I'm good."

"A'ight then, you free to go."

***

When Husain reached the parking lot, there was no one waiting for him. Afraid that he'd been let out by mistake, Husain left the premises walking. He noted a black Volvo coming down Rock Road. It passed him creeping at a sluggish pace, with windows tinted heavily. Paranoid, he turned to look behind him, and saw the Volvo making a U-turn. Rock Road was a long road with nothing but grass on both sides. There was nowhere for Husain to go, so he just stopped and waited to see who was creeping in the suspicious vehicle. Knowing that this could be his last moment on earth, his heart rate increased. The car pulled alongside of him and rolled the passenger window down.

"Get in." Husain peered into the car and saw that it was his father.

"Right on time," Husain stated, then hopped in the car, smiling, happy to see his father.

"Wassup? You a'ight? You hungry?" Khafre asked.

"Yeah, I'm starvin'! Let's go by Chic-fil-A." Husain rubbed his stomach.

"A'ight."

"How you knew I was gettin' out?" questioned Husain, not knowing if he'd been bailed out or if the detective had pulled some strings to get him out.

"I got'chu out. You think I'ma just let'chu sit in there and rot?"

"Thank you, pops. I thought it was over for the kid," asserted Husain, rubbing his hand over his deep waves.

"I'll neva leave you in a spot like that." Khafre pulled through Chic-fil-A's drive-thru and let Husain order his food. When the food was passed on into the car, Husain tried to ravish it but Khafre stopped him.

"What'chu doin', pops?" Husain looked at his father, confused.

"Hold up." Khafre opened the center console and grabbed a pre-rolled blunt. I want'chu to smoke this wit'me." Khafre smiled.

"I'on smoke, pop."

"Eventually, you will. Might as well smoke ya first one wit'cha pops."

"You serious?"

"Hell yeah! Smoke one wit' me."

"A'ight," Husain agreed, placing his food on the floor.

"That's what I'm talkin' bout. Vibe wit'cha pops." Khafre headed across the south bridge and pulled into a beach known as "The River." It got its name because it had no waves, only currents that moved like a river. Khafre backed in next to an Altima and cut the ignition off.

"So, how was it in there? You was holding shit down?" Khafre asked, then put flame to the blunt.

"Maaan! Pops, Rock Road is a hell hole, but'chu know, I held it down. I had to patch a few niggaz up, they press charges on me."

108

"N'all!" Khafre took a pull from the blunt and passed it to Husain.

"Yeah, I still gotta see if the state gone pick up the charges." Husain hit the blunt, held the smoke in then exhaled. "Where Hassan and Assata?" Husain asked, then hit the blunt again.

"Hassan wit' Lee Lee, and Assata's with her grandma. I didn't tell'em you was comin' home. I wanted to surprise 'em."

"I know they gone lose they mind when they see me," exclaimed Husain, laughing, now feeling the effect of the high grade weed.

"How you feelin'?"

"I'm high as hell, pops," Husain said, wiping his face repeatedly as if it would wipe the highness away.

"I see that you keep gigglin' and shit." Husain laughed again.

"All bullshit aside, stop laughin' and shit, so I can talk to you." Husain stopped laughing and paid attention to his father.

"Wassup, pop?" Khafre hit the blunt before speaking.

"You know I didn't want this life for you and yo' brother. I didn't want this for y'all but once you made up yo' mind to grab my pistol and shoot them three boys, I know it was no turning back." Husain tried his best to focus on what his father was saying, but he was high out his mind.

"You came from a bloodline of real killaz. Everybody's family has its flaws. We have our flaws but no matter the situation, no matter the odds, we all remained solid." Khafre had Husain's full attention now.

"Solid niggaz may not live forever, but pussy niggas don't live at all," Khafre philosophized.

"What'chu sayin', pop?"

"A real nigga only dies once."

"Huh?" Khafre exhaled seethingly before speaking.

"How the fuck you tell on a bitch!" Husain's heart rate increased.

"What?"

"How yo let a bitch remain solid but'chu fold?"

"It ain't like that, pop," Husain tried to explain.

"Shut the fuck up while I'm talkin'." Khafre had never spoken to Husain in this manner. Knowing that he'd let his hero down, tears fell from his eyes freely.

"Tasha could have told on you but she fuck wit'chu. Knowing she was facing twenty years for driving, she still remained solid. I salute her for that. Now, ain't no way in hell I was gone let'chu tell on her. I pulled some strings to get'chu out of there. I paid somebody to manipulate the computer. They gone prolly catch on to it so I gotta spot I'ma put'chu in in Atlanta. When you get there stay ya ass inside. Everything you need is in there. You hear me?" Husain nodded in shame.

"I can't hear you, police ass nigga!" Tears fell more rapidly at the sound of his father's remark.

"Come on, pop. Don't thug me like that," cried Husain.

"I got's to, police ass nigga! I want'chu to feel it, kuz you played! You tripped out bad, man!" yelled Khafre, pointing a finger at Husain's temple.

"Maan, pop—I love you, man. Please don't talk to me like that. Please."

"I love you too, nigga! But'chu hurt me. I'on want'chu 'round me right na! Get out, nigga walk home!" Khafre demanded through clenched teeth.

"Pop?" Husain muttered with the look of a battered soul.

"Get out!" Husain reached for the door handle.

"Husain!" Husain turned to look back at his father and found himself gazing at a FN 509 with a suppressor on it.

Fop! Khafre hit Husain right between the eyes, slumping him immediately. Slumped over in the passenger seat, Khafre hit his son four more times. He then lit his blunt and smoked it with tears falling from his eyes. When the blunt was finished, he got out of the Volvo, and hopped into the Altima that was parked next to him. Khafre had killed a lot of close relatives who crossed him, but killing Husain pained him the most.

Chapter Twenty-Four

Gang Paraphernalia

Three days later, Husain's body was found in the Volvo by an officer who was patrolling the beach checking license plates. The Volvo was reported stolen, so the officer called it in. When they found Husain's body, it had already started to decompose. He had a hole in his face and four more in his back. After searching the vehicle, the red rag that Khafre had gotten from the voodoo priest in Haiti was found in between the driver's seat, and the console. Khafre had lost his protection.

"Daddy. Husain hasn't called in like three days. Did he call you?" questioned Assata worried.

"No, baby girl. He might be in the hole."

"What hole?"

"When you do something wrong, they put you in a room by yourself. That's called the hole."

"Oh, but can't he use the phone still?"

"Depends, baby," Khafre replied apprehensively.

"On what?" Khafre's phone rang before he could answer Assata's question.

"Hold on, baby," he insisted, putting his hand up. "Hello?" Khafre answered.

"Hey, it's me. We need to talk!" Ketta said.

"Wassup?" asked Khafre, playing ignorant to the reason she was calling.

"In person."

"Where you at?"

"In front of your house."

"A'ight, I'm on my way out there." *Click!*

"Who was that, daddy?"

"My detective friend," Khafre admitted.

Assata grabbed Khafre's hand before he got up to leave.

"Tell her I said hi," said Assata with a heart melting smile.

"I got'cha, baby girl." Khafre kissed Assata on her forehead, then got up and headed outside. Expecting to see Ketta in her undercover car, he stopped in his tracks when he saw her sitting in a 2022 Mercedes-Benz G63 AMG black on black. Khafre admired the beautiful machine as he made his way to the passenger side and got in.

"Wassup, ma? Nice wheels."

"Thank you."

"My daughter said hey."

"Really?"

"Yeah."

"Tell her I said, hi."

"Will do."

"Listen, they found Husain dead." Ketta gave her words time to sink in and observed Khafre's reactions. He looked her in her eyes before speaking.

"Oh yeah?" Ketta was appalled at Khafre's response.

"Yeah, they found him at the beach, in a car, with a bullet in his head."

"Damn, that's fucked up," Khafre replied, turning his head away from her and gazing out of the window. Ketta shook her head in disbelief.

"If you'll kill yo' own son, I can only imagine what'chu'll do to me."

"I'on know what'chu speakin' on. You trippin'."

"Okay, I hear you. But how you gone explain that red flag you always be wearing being found in the car? The same car your son was found in." Khafre checked his right pocket and noticed that it was missing. He knew right then that he was no longer protected.

"He must have took it before going to jail," Khafre tried to explain.

"Even if that was the case, which I'm certain that it's not, it would have been confiscated as gang paraphernalia." Ketta shook her head again in disbelief. "You know their gon' to run a DNA test on that flag, right? What happens when only your DNA comes back conclusive?" Khafre turned and faced Ketta with worry painted all over his face. "I'm here to help you. How can I help you if you keep lying to me? You know how much I love you, nigga? I put my job on the line for you kuz I love the fuck out'chu! I ain't never met a nigga like you, and I'm not tryin' to lose you no time soon! You hear me?" Khafre wasn't sure if Ketta was wearing a wire up until that point. He knew now that he could trust her.

"I love you too, ma." Khafre shook his head from right to left as tears fell from his eyes. "It wasn't no way in hell I was gone let my son tell on Tasha. I couldn't let that be written in stone and stain my family's legacy." Ketta wiped the tears from Khafre's face.

"I hear you and I understand you. I got'chu baby, don't fret about nothin'." Ketta put her index finger under Khafre's chin and kissed him tenderly.

"You hear me?" questioned Ketta. Khafre nodded as he began to see Ketta in a different light. She was reminding him of Nilya.

"I hear you," Khafre stated.

"Okay, baby, I'ma call later," said Ketta. Khafre kissed her once more, then headed back inside.

Once inside, he called Hassan and Assata in the living room to deliver the devastating news, excluding the fact that he was the culprit behind their pain. Hassan and Assata both took it the hardest. On that cold summer night, a piece of them both died with Husain.

Chapter Twenty-Five

Big Daddy

"Hey, Roger. You're lookin' incredibly handsome today," Ketta flirted with an abundance of cleavage showing. Roger cleared his throat, obviously taken aback by Ketta's actions.

"Um—hi, detective," he replied nervously.

"Roger," Ketta stated, seductively placing her hand through the caged window and placing it on Roger's hand.

"Yes, detective." He could not believe that Ketta was actually touching him.

Roger was a black geeky type of guy, and the chances of a woman as beautiful as Ketta giving him some play was slim to none.

"I need you to do me a favor," Ketta said, grabbing the pen that was used to sign into the evidence room and putting the whole pen in her mouth slowly. Roger reached awkwardly and spilled his coffee all over his desk.

"Are you okay?" Ketta asked, knowing it was a rhetorical question.

"Ahh—ye, yeah. I'm fine," Roger lied, pushing his bifocals closer to his face. He then grabbed a gang of paper towels, and began to clean the desk off.

"So, ahh—What can I do for you, detective?"

"Please, call me Ketta," she exclaimed, grabbing his hand again.

"Oh, okay. What can I do for you, Ketta?"

"How would you like to take me out tonight?"

"Me?"

"Yes, you, big daddy. Me and you."

"Oh, umm—sure, I would love that," Roger admitted, smiling as a miniature tent formed in his pants.

"All you have to do is buzz me into the evidence room and I'm all yours, big daddy.

"Well, that's easy. All you have to do is sign in." Ketta stepped back out of the view of the camera, went under the skirt of her business suit and pulled her thongs off. She balled them up in her hand, walked back up to the caged window and handed them to Roger. While Roger was pre-cuming on himself, Ketta grabbed the login sheet, and forged the signature of another detective. Roger was so sunken into Ketta's hypnosis, that he didn't even check the log-in sheet. He buzzed her in, then sat at his desk and inhaled the scent of Ketta's nectar repeatedly. Ketta went in and grabbed Khafre's red flag out of evidence. When she returned, she caught Roger smelling her thongs.

"Don't worry, big daddy, you'll get the real thing tonight. Pick me up at nine-thirty," she instructed before leaving.

"See you then," Roger retorted, smiling goofy.

***

Ketta rode Roger in the driver's seat of his '98 Ford Explorer, like an Arabian thoroughbred at a derby. Instead of going out on an actual date, she decided to skip the bullshit and just fuck the shit out of Roger.

"This what the fuck you wanted, ana?" Ketta taunted through clenched teeth while rocking back in forth rapidly.

"Oh, my lord," moaned Roger as he held Ketta's fat ass and drooled on her breast.

"N'all nigga, don't call on the lord! Say my fuckin' name!"

"Oh God, Ketta. Yes!"

"What the fuck I say? Huh?" Ketta switched motions and began to gyrate hard and deep on Roger's shaft.

"Ketta baby, don't stop!" begged Roger, his eyes wide like a fiend.

116

"I can't fuckin' hear you, nigga! Ketta switched up again, and began to bounce up and down on Roger's dick, causing the truck to rock with proliferation.

"Oh Ketta, I think I love you!" Roger cried as his body began jerking awkward from cumming. Ketta bounced faster and harder until she climaxed, slowing her motion down while gripping the headrest of the driver's seat.

"I love you too, big daddy," she moaned seductively, unwrapping her arms from around the seat and placing a micro-compact 9mm Taurus to Roger's temple.

"Thanks for the nut, baby." *Boc!* Roger never felt a thing. His brain matter splattered all over Ketta's face and breast. Before fucking Roger, Ketta had placed her jacket over the driver's seat that concealed her weapon. She decided to give Roger some pussy before killing him. After getting dressed, she grabbed a gas can from the seat that Roger didn't question her about when she got in his vehicle, and poured gas all over him and his truck. Ketta then lit the truck on fire, and left it to burn on Taylor's Creek ditch banks. Her whip was parked around the corner. She hopped in and slipped away under the moon.

Chapter Twenty-Six

Murda Courtesy

"You don't have to worry about being questioned for Husain's murder," Ketta said, pulling the red rag from her glove box and handing it to Khafre. He gazed at her ambivalently, not understanding why this woman was putting everything on the line for him, especially after killing his own son.

"I love you and I appreciate 'chu," said Khafre.

"It's okay, baby, I love you more. I told you I got'chu." Khafre exhaled before speaking.

"When we first started this shit, my only intention was to manipulate 'chu to handle my bidness. I was just gone use you, but'chu captured my heart in the process." Ketta nodded understandably. "After losing my soul mate to the streets, I thought that I was incapable of loving again. I grew a callous on my heart, but you've peeled it away, layer by layer. I love you with all four chambers of my heart, and that's past forever!" said Khafre.

"I love you too, baby," replied Ketta, wiping the tears from her face. After sharing a tender kiss, a green Genesis pulled next to Ketta's rental car. "I'll be right back, daddy," said Ketta, grabbing a duffle bag from the back seat and exiting the vehicle. She approached the driver's door as the window was being lowered.

"Wassup, New York?" asked Ketta, handing him the duffle bag. New York was a guard who moved to Florida from Brooklyn to work out of Rock Road's county jail.

"Shit's been real crazy for me! They've been askin' a lot of questions. I'm under investigation!" New York cried, opening the duffle bag and seeing stacks of blue hunids. He smiled and zipped the bag back up.

"That's a hunid racks. While you're under investigation, go on a vacation. Enjoy yourself," Ketta encouraged. She looked around and made sure no one was around or peeking out of the *Pink Apartments* on Avenue T. Somebody was always watching, and she wanted to be sure no one witnessed this transaction.

"You don't think that would raise suspicion?" asked New York eyebrows raised.

"Yeah, you right." *Boc! Boc! Boc! Boc!* Ketta had drawn her weapon swiftly and let off four shots in New York's face. The shots echoed loudly in the wee-hour of the morning. She reached in the vehicle, grabbed the duffle bag that was now painted with brain matter, and hopped back in the car with Khafre.

"If you was gone kill the nigga anyway why did you even hand him the money?" Khafre questioned. Ketta pulled off.

"I had to see how much he knew about the investigation. Plus, he prolly neva seen a hunid-thousand before in his life. I granted him that before death," explained Ketta. Khafre smiled at Ketta's gangsta.

"Murda courtesy, huh?"

"You betta believe it," Ketta boasted. They both laughed as they slipped away from the murder scene unnoticed.

***

Instead of having a funeral for Husain, Khafre decided to have him cremated. He waited until sunset, so he could spread his son's ashes in the same place that he spread his father's—in the ocean. Khafre was accompanied by Ketta, Shantel, Hassan, Tasha, Lee Lee, Assata, and Wolly. The only one who cried was Shantel. Everybody else had come to accept the loss. When Khafre spread Hussain's ashes, Hassan and Assata released doves, and watched them fly towards the divine architecture that the supreme architect had illustrated across the sky.

"I'ma catch you in the life after," Hassan mumbled to himself.

"I love you, bra! Assata yelled.

"Rest easy," Khafre added, then put flame to a blunt.

"Sorry for your loss, Khafre," Wolly sympathized, hugging Khafre's neck.

"Respect," he replied, blowing smoke from his nose.

"Let me hit that reefer," Shantel stated, grabbing the blunt from Khafre's hand.

"I'm sorry," Tasha added, hugging Khafre.

"Thank you. Listen, I respect you keeping shit solid. You could have easily told and been free. If you ever need anything, call me or come by."

"Yes, sir. My lawyer told me charges should be gettin' dismissed soon," Tasha informed.

"That's wassup."

"So do you know who killed 'em?" Tasha asked curiously.

"Not yet, I'm workin' on it," lied Khafre.

"Babe, we got company," Ketta whispered in Khafre's ear. "I think it's the Feds," said Ketta. Khafre turned and saw two suspicious white men that looked completely out of place.

"Fuck they want wit' me," Khafre asked, shooting a bird at 'em.

"I gotta go, babe. I'ma call you later," Ketta announced before leaving. Everybody else turned to see who Khafre was telling to fuck off, and joined him.

"Suck my dick, pussy ass Krakaz!" yelled Khafre, then turned back to the beautiful sunset and continued to smoke his blunt.

Chapter Twenty-Seven

I'm Hit

Three Summers Later—

Assata was behind the wheel of a stolen Acura, spinning blocks with Hassan. Ever since Husain was murdered, Assata and Hassan had been on a rampage. It was a gang of accusations about who had really killed Husain, and since no one could be properly accused, Hassan and Assata terrorized both sides of town.

"Aye, spin through Bethany Court. I heard it's thick out there," Hassan stated with twin Springfield Hellcat 9mm's on his lap.

"Yea, a'ight, I got'cha," Assata replied, turning Mozzy up on the sound system.

—These niggas kill me with this killin' shit / If that's the case, then why I still exist? Talk to me, huh? / We usin' green ones over silver tips / I was one of the ones before you did a skit, simmer down / I was one of the ones you called for pay, oh niggas dissin now? / Really one of the ones to place a call and have 'em sit you down / You seen what happen to ya partner, bitch, go dig him out / And if they get my partner bail I'm goin to go get him out—

Assata made a right on 13th Street and Avenue Q, then made a left on a back street that ran between Bethany's Court and the LP (Lil' Projects). Hassan noted mini crowds standing in sections on porches of young women who were on Section 8. He moved over to the window behind Assata and gripped both pistols. When Assata stopped in front of the first crowd, Hassan came out of the window hittin' with both pistols. *Boc! Boc! Boc! Boc! Boc! Boc!* Bullets ripped through flesh, causing bodies to spin before dropping. The other crowd of people scattered and fled for their lives. Assata mashed the gas, almost hitting a few with the vehicle. Hassan came out of the window again.

"Don't run na!" *Boc! Boc! Boc! Boc! Boc! Boc!* "Wassup na?" *Boc! Boc! Boc! Boc! Boc! Boc!* More bodies dropped, men and women laid sprawled out on the pavement and grass. Assata got on the gas and made a right on Avenue N to head back across town.

"Spin around one mo'e time," Hassan announced, changing his clips out.

"You sho'?" Assata asked, worried that the police were probably on their way.

"Hell yeah, I'm sho," he said, cocking both pistols. Assata spinned the block again and saw bodies stretched, some with life still in them.

"Y'all act like y'all don't know who killed my fuckin' brother! Huh?" Hassan yelled through clenched teeth and attempted to hang out of the window and fire but someone did before he could.

Kak! Kak! Kak! Kak! Kak! Kak! Kak! 67.2 rounds tore through the Acura like butter from the other side of the street.

"Aaahh! Shit!" yelled Assata, pushing the gas to the floor.

Kak! Kak! Kak! Kak! Kak! Kak!

"I'm hit!" Assata yelled as she barely made it around the corner, escaping death. A choppa bullet had grazed her on the arm, causing blood to pour out rapidly. She noticed that she didn't hear Hassan respond to her being hit. Assata turned around and seen Hassan stretched out on the back seat holding his stomach. The sight of Hassan pushing his organs back inside of his stomach sent Assata into a state of panic.

122

"Hassan! Hassan! Hold on, bra, don't die on me! I need you, don't die on me!" yelled Assata as tears fell from her face rapidly. Once she was a couple of blocks away from the crime scene, the engine in the Acura died. The 67.2 rounds had killed the engine. Assata moved quickly, hopping out of the vehicle and opening the backdoor. She took Hassan's pistols and hid them in some bushes nearby. When she came back, Hassan was barely conscious. She grabbed him up under his arms and pulled him out of the car. Hassan laid between Assata's legs with his back turned towards her.

"Please don't leave me, bra," Assata cried with her arms wrapped around Hassan. She placed her hands on top of his, helping him keep his organs inside of his stomach.

"You all I got left. Please, don't die on me." Assata kissed Hassan on his cheek.

"Please don't die!"

Chapter Twenty-Eight

Maleficence

Tears fell rapidly from Assata's eyes as she gripped the steering wheel of a Benz that she'd stolen from the hospital. The driver had carelessly left his keys in the ignition before going into the hospital. After hearing the doctor explain the critical condition of Hassan, Assata's vision was clouded with blood. She went home and grabbed her father's modified AK-47. It was dressed with a box clip that held 25 rounds, a green beam, and flashlight that traveled 100 yards.

"God! Why does it feel like I'm being punished? Everything that I love dies! What the fuck did I do to you? Huh?" Assata questioned, her bottom lip quivering. "Aaaahh!" Assata yelled and banged her fist on the steering wheel. "I'mma show you that I'm built for whatever the fuck you send my way!" Assata made a right on 13th and Edgewood Terrace, creeping past the same street that held the shooters who'd put Hassan in critical condition.

Assata saw that the street was crowded with killaz, trappaz and thots, as if a massacre didn't occur two days ago. She drove twenty more yards, then parked on the side of the road. "A'ight, mothafukaz," Assata stated through clenched teeth, grabbing the AK from the backseat and hopping out. After cutting the light on that rested on the side of the rifle, Assata rounded the building of Bethany's Court, holding the AK like a firehose. Thinking Assata was the police, a few people ran throwing their dope and guns, but still managed to get caught in Assata's violence. So many rounds were fired, that the intended prey was under the impression that there was more than one shooter. Assata held the assault rifle like her father had taught her and waved it from one side of the street to the other in an artistic rhythm, like a brush to a canvas. Bodies dropped on both sides, vehicles were Swiss-cheesed, and chunks of cheap cement detached away from the project buildings. In awe of the destruction that the jobs were administrating, Assata's eyes averted from the flame that was jumping out the front of the rifle back to the bodies that were dropping. After spraying close to one hundred and fifty rounds, Assata stopped firing and disappeared around the building, her back hugging the wall. Ten seconds later, the ones who managed to take cover began to move around and check on their comrades and loved ones. Mothers and girlfriends screamed in agony at the horror that lay before them. Just when they attempted to fathom the thought that shit couldn't possibly get worse, Assata rounded the building again, and fired everything left in the box clip. She then hopped back in the Benz and peeled off away from the scene.

***

Khafre sat on the trunk of his Yenko Camaro, smoking a Grabba leaf filled with purple diesel as he pondered Hassan's condition, and Assata's whereabouts. He'd searched the entire hospital for Assata, but to no avail. Picking up his phone to call her again, he was caught off guard by a Benz abruptly pulling in his driveway. Khafre reached for his pistol, but released his grip once he'd seen that it was Assata.

"Assata!" Khafre yelled, eyebrows creased. Assata kicked the driver's door open and stepped out holding the AK-47 with both of her tiny hands. She stood by the vehicle, holding the rifle, trembling as tears descended down both sides of her distorted face. Gazing in his daughter's eyes, Khafre knew that look all too well. It was the same look he had after losing Shenida, Nilya, and his father. It was the look of maleficence...the look of vengeance. It was the same look Khafre had after his first kill. Khafre slid off the trunk of his car and made his way towards Assata.

"Daddy I—"

"Shh! Khafre silenced her and wrapped his arms around her. "It's gone be a'ight, baby, I promise." Khafre could feel her entire body shaking. "Listen. Go inside, take a shower, put'cha clothes in a bag and I'll get'em when I come back. Try to get some rest, ya hear me?" Assata nodded in agreement. Khafre kissed her forehead, grabbed the rifle from her and hopped in the stolen Benz. He made his way over to Taylor's Creek and dumped them both where they'd never be found.

Chapter Twenty-Nine

Celestial Forces

Khafre entered the house in a conflictual state. He didn't want his fourteen-year-old daughter catching a body, but in retrospect he understood it. He'd been in her shoes before and sympathized with her reasoning. Khafre knew that Assata was acting out of her loyalty to her brother. Khafre grabbed a half of blunt from the ashtray on a coffee table, lit it and headed to Assata's room. When he entered, she was curled up in a fetal position. "Assata," Khafre stated mildly. She turned over and faced her father.

"You a'ight?" he asked, joining her in her *HiCan* bed and turning on the 70-inch home theater screen.

"No," Assata replied barely above a whisper. Khafre wiped the tears from her face that fell so freely, then turned the TV on CNN.

"It's okay to be not okay, baby girl, but 'chu gotta climb outta this state of depression sooner than later," Khafre stated, pulling from his blunt.

"I just feel like, God is punishing me, daddy."

"Sit up," Khafre demanded. Assata did as she was told.

"Listen, baby girl. God is not punishing you. I used to feel the same way, but that's not the case. God—the Creator—created this world to operate off of universal law. A divine law called cause and effect."

"What that mean, daddy?"

"It means that every action has a reaction."

"So basically, whatever you do it has its consequences?"

"Exactly," Khafre said.

126

"I hear you, but I haven't done anything wrong to deserve this. We lost Mom, Husain, and it look like we might lose Hassan too," cried Assata as her eyes began to water again.

"Stop all that damn cryin'! Real warriors don't cry! The only way to mourn a fallen soldier is to pick up the fallen weapon. You've done that already, and I respect and love you for it. It's true, you didn't do nothin' to deserve this pain, but yo' mother, Husain, and Hassan—they did something that caused their unfortunate circumstances. You can't escape celestial forces, baby girl. Everybody gets dealt with accordingly for their actions, and sometimes other people suffer from the actions of others. That's just how the world works. You hear me?" Khafre asked, then re-lit his blunt.

"Yes, daddy, I hear you. I understand, but I still don't like it," Assata admitted.

"As long as you understand it," Khafre replied.

Exhausted, Assata laid her head on her father's shoulder. Moments later, her demonstration was illustrated across the TV screen. The news reporter was calling the onslaught a massacre. Six people were pronounced dead on the scene, while others—men, women, and kids— suffered near-death injuries. No suspects had been apprehended. At the end of the segment, a video clip was shown of Assata in bloody clothing being asked about what happened to Hassan, and if she knew who did it? She declined to speak.

"So how you feel seeing yo' drill session make the news?" Implied Khafre.

Assata shrugged.

"Honestly, I feel like more people should have died. I done lost too much blood to feel sorry for someone else. I'm just getting started!" Assata asserted.

"Aaah shit," muttered Khafre. "Here, you want to hit this shit?" Khafre asked, passing the blunt to his daughter.

"Why not?" Assata replied and grabbed the blunt. She tried her best to relax as she smoked her first blunt with her father.

Chapter Thirty

I'ma Gangsta

A peculiar stench awoke Khafre from an extremely graphic dream. When he became fully conscious of his surroundings, he noticed that his Armani t-shirt was soaked with sweat. The scene of Nilya being killed replayed in his dream, except this time, when he tried to fire, his gun was inoperable. He helplessly watched the killers flee the scene, and when he tried to open Nilya's door, it wouldn't open. Nilya's blood began to flood the vehicle and leak from the car. What Khafre thought to be the smell of Nilya's blood was actually the smell of a high graded strand of weed.

"Nilya," Khafre muttered to himself before removing his soaked shirt. He wiped his hand over his face, then got up and followed the delightful odor that led him to the living room.

"Good morning," Lee Lee stated dryly.

"Wassup wit it?" Khafre said, noting that Lee Lee seemed dejected.

"I'm just a lil' stressed, ya know," Lee Lee admitted.

"Stress will kill ya. Don't worry yaself, Hassan going be a'ight. You hear me?"

"Yes, sir," Lee Lee replied, praying that he was right.

"Morning, daddy," Assata said, handing Khafre a blunt.

"I see you addicted already," Khafre claimed, grabbing the blunt and having a seat next to Assata.

"Don't do me, dad. I needed it. It calms me."

"This shit woke me outta my sleep. What this is?"

"Green monkey," asserted Lee Lee.

"Green monkey, huh?" Khafre hit the blunt and coughed from the potency.

"Pass that before you hurt'cha self," advised Lee Lee, reaching for the blunt.

"Get this shit. How long you been here?" asked Khafre, passing Lee Lee the blunt.

"I got dropped off like an hour ago. Me and Assata just been in here talking 'bout Hassan."

"Yeah, we wanna go sit with him," added Assata.

"A'ight, give me a lil' minute. I gotta hop in the shower."

"We'll be ready," Assata assured. Khafre disappeared and returned an hour later. The trio hopped in his Mercedes EQG and headed to Lawnwood Medical Center.

***

While Assata and Lee Lee engaged in small talk, Khafre watched his rear-view mirror incessantly. The moment he pulled out of his driveway., it appeared that he was being followed. Khafre grabbed his Glock-22 from his Bulgari sweats and placed it on his lap with his finger on the trigger.

"Everything okay, daddy?" Assata questioned, observing her father's movement.

"Yea, baby girl. Everything velvet," Khafre assured, making a left off 25th Street and turning into the hospital. The vehicle that was trailing him kept straight. Khafre relaxed a little and found a parking spot. The trio exited the car and headed inside.

"You sure all is well?" Assata asked again, her expression studious.

"Yeah, baby," I thought I'd seen somethin'. We good though."

130

"I'll appreciate it if you put me on point next time. Don't do me like that. You know what I just experienced with Hassan," Assata stated, face tightening with emotion.

"I didn't wanna worry you, baby girl, but I hear you and I feel you," he replied. Khafre put his arm around Assata before entering Hassan's room. Surprisingly, Shantel was by Hassan's bedside, her eyes puffy and red.

"Wassup, Ma?" said Khafre, hugging Shantel's neck.

"Hey, baby. I been here all night. My baby still ain't open his eyes yet," cried Shantel, rubbing Hassan's hand.

"He gone wake up, momma."

"Hey, grandma."

"Hey, Ms. Shantel." Assata and Lee Lee spoke in tandem.

"Hey, y'all," Shantel replied dryly. "The doctor said that half of his stomach was removed, one of his lungs collapsed, and he might not be able to walk again. A bullet grazed him on the side of his head too." Tears fell from Shantel's face. Her crying caused Assata's and Lee Lee's eyes to water.

"You ain't tired of everybody around you dying? Huh? You died yourself, Khafre! I was right there when they pronounced you dead! Enough is enough, man! When you gone change yo' life?" said Shantel.

"I understand you frustrated and hurt, but don't act like you don't know what we come from. I'ma Gangsta! You know what come wit' this shit. We all do. Na. Ion mean to ruffle ya feathers, but we both know ain't nobody living forever. So, while you here, it's eat or get ate. I love you, momma, but don't never come at me like I'm the reason my son laid up in that bed. Assata!"

"Yes, daddy?"

"Call me if he wakes up. I'm out!" Khafre asserted before leaving. Tears fell more rapidly from the wells of Shantel's eyes.

Chapter Thirty-One

I Fucked Up

When Khafre left the hospital, he was conflicted. He'd never spoken to his mother in that manner, but it felt essential at the moment. Before he could reach his phone, it started to ring.

"Yea!"

"What's up, bae?" Ketta asked.

"Just dropped Assata and Lee Lee off at the hospital."

"And how is Hassan?"

"He still ain't open his eyes yet. He'll wake up in a minute though. He got that warrior blood in him," Khafre stated assuringly while glancing in his rearview.

"Yea, he'll pull through," Ketta agreed.

"Da fuck," mumbled Khafre, making a left on 25th Avenue M.

"What's the matter, daddy?" Ketta asked, concerned.

"I been getting' followed all mornin'. I'm finna hop out and flip that shit," Khafre threatened.

"So, you been getting followed all morning?"

"Somebody followed me this morning on the way to hospital. Na somebody on my tail na."

"The same car from this morning?"

"N'all, this shit different."

"Khafre, don't do nothing stupid. That's probably the Feds, daddy."

"Can't be. I ain't been doing nothing," said Khafre, pulling into the park in the projects.

"Think about it, bae. If it was jackboyz or hitmen, they would have made a move by now. If it's a different car, it's the feds, baby. Trust me!" Ketta exclaimed, worried about Khafre safety.

"I got it, bae. I'ma call you back. *Click!* Khafre pulled in front of the restrooms. He noticed the same Ford 500 backing in two parking spots down. Ketta called his phone back-to-back, but he ignored it. He grabbed his Jeff Hamilton hoodie off the passenger seat, put it on, then reached under his seat and grabbed his modified Glock-22. It had a green beam, and a 50-round extension with a switch on it. Khafre cuffed the Glock and headed in the restroom. Two minutes later, he exited the restroom and headed straight for the Ford 500. When he was ten feet away from the car, he waved with his left hand to disguise hostility. He couldn't determine who was in the vehicle, but the two who were inside waved back. Khafre pulled his weapon from his hoodie and sprayed the passenger's window. He then walked in front of the car and proceeded to spray through the front windshield. Both bodies bounced around chaotically from the impact and the attempt to dodge the shots that were raining through the windshield. Khafre stopped shooting, hopped on the hood of the Ford, and sprayed the rest of the clip into both bodies. Trails of gun smoke lingered in the air. Khafre hopped off the hood of the car and opened the driver's door. Both men of European descent were coughing up blood and chasing their breath. Within seconds they both succumbed from their wounds. When Khafre saw what was on the hip of the driver, he knew life as he knew it will never be the same.

***

Not being able to get in contact with Khafre had Ketta panic-stricken. She had been calling for an hour straight only to be aggravated by the voicemail.

"Damn, nigga, pick up the fucking phone," Ketta muttered through clenched teeth. She tried calling again but got the same results. Ketta placed her phone in her Fendi clutch and entered her home. After securing her front door, she drew her service weapon and maneuvered through the house with diligence. Ketta lived alone, so there was no reason for her lights to be on. She always made it her business to cut them off before leaving. Someone was in her house. Ketta cleared each room as she made it down the long spacious hallway. When she made it to the end, she rounded the corner and entered her room.

Boc! Boc!

Khafre examined the two holes in the wall, then looked back at Ketta.

"Khafre?" Ketta asked, contrition in her voice. Khafre took a pull on his blunt.

"You just gone blow my head off?" Khafre said, then exhaled smoke from his nose.

"Khafre, what the fuck? I been calling you! Why you ain't pick up? What happened?" Ketta asked, using her hands for emphasis.

"I threw my phone away. You might wanna do the same."

"Wassup, baby?"

"I fucked up. I fucked up bad this time," Khafre admitted, feeling defeated. Afraid of what Khafre would

134

say next, Ketta's body was instantly wrapped in a sheet of terror. She took a seat next to Khafre on her bed.

"Tell me what happened."

"You were right. The people who were following me were the feds." Khafre took another pull from his blunt.

"Okay, so—how did you realize I was right?"

"I wet their shit up. Stood on the hood and sprayed all through the windshield and shit." Khafre shook his head in disappointment. "I killed 'em. When I snatched the door open, I saw the federal badge on their hip. It's over for me."

"Ffffuck! Damn, daddy. I tried to tell you, but don't trip." Tears fell from Ketta's face, knowing the immense heat that was coming down. "I know somebody who makes fake ID's and can getcha a passport. Just chill here for now until you decide where you wanna go."

"N'all, they're going to come here. They prolly had my phone tapped."

"This phone is not in my name. Nobody in my workplace knows me as Ketta. My real name is Ketonna. You safe here," Ketta assured.

"They can just ping yo' location, right?"

"If it makes you feel better, I'll get rid of the phone."

"Yea, you do that. It's somethin' else I need you to do for me."

"Anything, baby."

"Look after Assata for me please."

"I gotcha, daddy," assured Ketta.

Chapter Thirty-Two

Emotionally Paralyzed

The next morning, Ketta awoke to a pleasant aroma. She stretched, then rolled over to put her arm around Khafre, but he wasn't there. Her stomach roared as the delightful smell of bacon continued to invade her nostrils. A smile spread across her face at the thought of Khafre cooking her breakfast in bed. Ketta climbed out of the bed and made her way down the hallway.

"Bae," Ketta called out seductively. "Bae, I know you hear me!"

When Ketta entered the kitchen, Khafre was nowhere to be found. She ran back down the hallway, checked both bathrooms, the one in her room inclusive, then headed back to the kitchen. The smell of bacon was still fresh in the air, so she figured Khafre couldn't been gone long. She finally noticed a plate laced with bacon, eggs, and a cup of *Simply Lemonade* with a note next to it. Ketta picked up the note and read it with trepidation.

Ketta,
It's apparent that my love for you is immeasurable. After losing my first love, I thought that I was incapable of loving another, but you changed that. The sacrifices that you've made for me, and mines has peeled away the callus from my heart. Your intentions are pure, and for that, I love you with all four chambers of my heart. I know the gravity of my situation, and I refuse to be a liability. That explains my absence, but you'll see me again... I promise! I have no distrust about leaving my daughter in your care. Just give her my love. Enjoy your breakfast.

Love Khafre

Ketta balled the letter up and fell into a mild panic attack. She couldn't fathom why Khafre didn't let her help him. Most importantly, she couldn't live with the fact that Khafre didn't give her the proper goodbye. Ketta placed her hands on the table and cried uncontrollably. Tears fell freely into the plate of food Khafre had fixed her.

***

After getting her emotions together, Ketta took a shower, got dressed then headed to the hospital. When she entered Hassan's room, he still hadn't woken up. Shantel, Lee Lee and Assata were still by his side.

"Hey, y'all," Ketta greeted. Everybody spoke in tandem. "Shantel, can I speak witchu for a minute?"

"Sure," Shantel replied just above a whisper and headed to the hallway behind Ketta. "What's going on?" questioned Shantel.

Ketta drew in a deep breath, then exhaled before speaking.

"Khafre in a precarious situation."

"What'chu mean?" Shantel retorted as her heart rate began to increase.

"The feds want 'em."

"Oh Lord," cried Shantel, placing a hand over her mouth.

"Yeah, he on the run as we speak."

"What happened?"

"I don't know. He didn't say," lied Ketta, not wanting Shantel to know that Khafre killed two federal officers.

"Well, why he didn't call me?" Shantel questioned, feeling some type of way.

"He thinks that his phone was tapped. So, he didn't wanna call you. He just showed up to my house, told me the feds were on him. Then he just left."

Shantel placed her hands on her hips and stared at the floor in a daze.

"Shit!" Shantel said and took off towards the elevator.

"Shantel!" Ketta called out, but Shantel ignored her and hurried into the elevator. Ketta sighed then headed back to Hassan's room.

"Assata, come here."

Assata made her way over to Ketta.

"Yes?"

"Yo' father wants you to come live with me for a while."

"What? Why?" Assata asked, her eyebrows creased.

"He had to go out of town for a while. The feds looking for him."

After everything Assata's been through, she wasn't even surprised. She was emotionally paralyzed.

"Okay," Assata replied.

Chapter Thirty-Three

Frozen

Shantel used the spare key that Khafre had given her and entered his home. The house was extremely quiet, and even though it was well furnished, it was a bit tainted due to Assata's negligence. Shantel headed straight for Khafre's room with her Goyard duffle bag and placed it on the bed. She then removed a picture of Nat Turner from the wall, and opened the safe that was concealed behind it.

"Damn!" exclaimed Shantel as she gazed at the two million dollars in cash, all blue-faced hundreds. She quickly transferred the money to the duffle bag and headed towards the front door. The moment she stepped foot in the living room, the front door was kicked in, followed by men bearing modified assault weapons and tactical gear.

"FBI! On the fucking ground now! Who else is in the house! Don't fuckin' move!"

Shantel's heart collapsed to her cervix as she made her way to the ground. Someone grabbed the duffle bag, another pointed a rifle at her head, while the rest maneuvered through the home.

"Who else is in the fucking house!"

"Nobody!" Shantel screamed, then urinated on herself.

"We're all clear!" yelled an ATF officer.

"Get her up and sit her on the couch," ordered a federal agent.

When Shantel was placed on the couch, tears were already falling from her eyes.

"Hello, Shantel. I'm agent Palaski, Federal Bureau of Investigations," Palaski stated jovially.

Shantel just sat in silence.

"Where were you taking this money?" Palaski asked, pointing to the duffle bag.

"Shantel remained silent.

"You were taking it to your son? Where is he?"

Still no response from Shantel.

"Your son killed two federal agents. He's in a world of trouble, so it's best you tell us his whereabouts. Do you want your son to die? If he doesn't turn himself in, my guys are going to see to it that he's brought in…in a body bag. You want that, Shantel?"

"We gotta arsenal!" one of the D.E.A. officers said, placing another duffle bag in front of Palaski.

When Palaksi looked in the bag, it contained a Draco, Mp-5 with a silencer, a M-10 with a box clip, a vest, and a modified Romanian AK.

"Well, looky here!" Palaski asserted, smirking diabolically. "Either you tell me where Khafre is, or you're being charged with money laundering and interstate commerce. The trafficking of assault weapons across state lines. Oh yea, and conspiracy."

"I want a lawyer," Shantel retorted.

"You sure? 'Cuz if you tell me where Khafre is, I'll let'chu go right now with no charges against you." Palaski tried to persuade.

"Lawyer!" Shantel stated firmly.

***

Unbeknownst to Shantel, the feds had raided her home and Khafre's simultaneously. They found another two hundred thousand, and copies of articles of organization for Khafre's yacht cleaning business. She became aware the next morning at bond hearing. By this being Shantel's first offense, the judge showed leniency and granted bond. Mercedes, who was Shantel's best

140

friend, posted her bail. Now Shantel was out and wearing an ankle monitor.

"Thank you so much, Cedes," exclaimed Shantel. "You know I gotta pay you back."

"No problem girl. You know I gotchu," Mercedes replied, pulling into Chase Bank.

"I'll be right back," Shantel said before exiting the car and heading into the bank.

"Hello, Ms. Sheffield, how are you today?" Sandy asked. Sandy was the bank teller. She had become accustomed to Shantel coming in every week depositing money.

"Hi, Sandy, I'm okay I guess," replied Shantel, handing the teller a check and her identification. After a few clicks on her computer, Sandy handed Shantel back the check.

"I'm sorry to inform you that your account has been frozen until further notice."

"Frozen? Why?" Shantel inquired.

"It appears to be a Federal Investigation. The money isn't technically gone. If you can prove where the money came from, then they'll unfreeze the account." Shantel exhaled deeply and rubbed her hand across her forehead.

"Okay, thank you, Sandy."

"I'm sorry," said Sandy.

Shantel left the bank devastated. Once back in the car, Mercedes could sense that something was wrong.

"What's wrong, friend?"

"Girl, they done froze my account," said Shantel as tears cascaded down her face. "I told Khafre this shit was gone happen. They took my money from my house. They took Khafre's money, and they froze our account. We ain't got no more money! How I'ma make it with no money?" Shantel cried solemnly.

Mercedes consoled Shantel, rubbing her back.

"It's okay friend. I'll take care of you, "Mercedes assured.

Chapter Thirty-Four
Blood Split

It had been a discouraging day for Ketta. After getting Assata settled in, she took a seat at her kitchen table, and scrolled down Facebook. Expecting to see the latest news on Khafre, Ketta was taken aback to see Shantel's face next to his. It stated that Khafre was under investigation for conspiracy and while under surveillance he killed two federal agents. He was also charged with being in possession of assault weapons, and money laundering. Shantel was charged with the same weapons and money laundering. All Ketta could do was shake her head. She made a mental note to go check on Shantel in the morning.

"Damn," muttered Ketta before getting up to grab a *Snapple* from the fridge. When she turned around, a hand was placed over her mouth. Her eyes grew wide, and her face froze in a visage of sheer terror.

"Shhh!" Khafre grabbed the *Snapple* from Ketta's hand, removed his hand from her mouth and placed a soft kiss on her bulbous lips. Ketta sighed as a single tear fell slowly from her right eye. Thinking that she would never see Khafre again had her in a conflicted state. She reciprocated, kissing Khafre deeply, stirring a torrid typhoon between her legs. Ketta gasped.

"Khafre," she whispered.

He shook his head from right to left, indicating that he didn't want to talk. Khafre then pushed her towards her room aggressively. Ketta obliged and power-walked to her room. When Khafre entered the room behind her, Ketta was lying on the bed panting, opening, and closing her legs, while gripping the bed spread.

"Khafre," Ketta whispered, pinching her nipples and biting her bottom lip.

Khafre closed the door behind him, then sat the *Snapple* on the dresser. He then removed his black

Givenchy t-shirt, placed his FN-509 on the dresser, and removed his sweats, and briefs.

"I need you, daddy," whined Ketta, rotating her hips, before removing her clothing abruptly.

Khafre grabbed the *Snapple*, popped the top, walked towards the edge of the bed, and motioned for Ketta to approach him. Ketta crawled to the edge of the bed seductively as her mouth watered. Khafre poured *Snapple* on his pulsating dick, then guided it into Ketta's mouth. Ketta moaned as she sucked and slurped the *Snapple* juice from Khafre's dick while looking into his eyes. He matched her stare while snarling through clenched teeth and gripping her head with his left hand. Not wanting to cum early, Khafre snatched his dick out her mouth and put the *Snapple* on the floor.

"Put that dick back in my mouth," Ketta cried.

Khafre grabbed her hair with his left hand and pushed his dick in her mouth aggressively, causing her to gag. He snatched it out her mouth again and yanked her head back. Ketta stuck her tongue out like a parched pit bull. Khafre spanked his dick on her tongue, rubbed it side to side, then pushed back into Ketta's mouth. After snatching out of her mouth again, Khafre grabbed his dick and spanked Ketta on the side of her face and neck, leaving traces of pre-cum.

"Yesss, put that dick on my face," Ketta moaned.

Ready to heat shit up, Khafre forced Ketta to turn around and lie face down, cheeks up. He grabbed the *Snapple* juice, then slapped Ketta on her right ass cheek. Ketta moaned and used both of her hands to spread her ass as wide as she could. Khafre poured juice into her asshole then sucked every drop out.

"Shhiit! Daddy, yesss!"

144

After pouring the rest of the juice between her ass, Khafre plunged his tongue in and out her ass while using his right middle index finger to manipulate her clit.

"Whooo! Sss! Whoo...Ssshit. Yes!" She cried, creaming all over Khafre's hand.

Khafre licked his hands clean, ran his tongue down her ass crack, then blew tenderly. Ketta shook with anticipation of penetration. Khafre stood and entered Ketta from behind. Her wet glue-like fit sent a chill throughout his body, causing him to grip her cotton soft ass cheeks like a pair of pliers.

"Ummm..." Ketta moaned as Khafre pushed deep down in her and held it there. He ground his pelvic bone against her ass cheeks, pulled out of her slowly, then dove deep back inside of her.

"Sss! Shit! Stop teasing me and beat this pussy!" Ketta encouraged, winding her hips. "Beat it!" she dared through clenched teeth.

Accepting the challenge, Khafre picked up his pace as the sound of her moaning and ass clapping against his pelvis created a familiar symphony.

"Haaa! Yesss—Sss—fuck me, nigga!" Ketta taunted, looking back at Khafre who was now growling, baring a grimacing expression. She threw her pussy back, matching him thrust for thrust.

"Shit!" Khafre finally spoke, unable to remain quiet, courtesy of Ketta's pussy walls contracting around his dick.

"I know, nigga! This pussy good na!" Ketta boasted as her pussy creamed and started smacking.

"Shut the fuck up!" Khafre demanded, pushing her head in the pillow, followed by rapid, deep, and intense strokes.

"Mmmm—Mmm!" Ketta's moans were muffled by the pillow she was biting.

"Ffffuucckk! I'm on my way!" Khafre announced, then growled as he came in Ketta's sopping pussy.

"Mmmm—Aaaaahhh!" Ketta groaned, climaxing simultaneously with Khafre. He snatched out of her dripping pussy and flipped her on her back. Attempting to eat her pussy, Ketta pushed him away and slipped out of the bed. She pushed Khafre in the bed, then mounted him eagerly.

"Give me this dick!" Ketta wiggled down on all inches, placing her hands on Khafre's chest, bouncing on his dick aggressively.

"That's it!" Ride that shit then!" Khafre moaned, gripping her fat ass cheeks.

Ketta bounced, grinding like a dance hall queen, then bounced again.

"Sss—Ooooww! I fucking love you, nigga! Ssshit!"

Not wanting to cum again, she hopped off Khafre's drenched dick and put it deep in her throat.

"Sssshiit!" Khafre attempted to crawl backwards, but Ketta locked her leg around his and had a death grip on his dick. Ketta moaned as she sucked and slurped him vivaciously.

"Ffuuck! Bitch, I love you!" Khafre cried, gripping the sheets.

"Mmmm!" Ketta moaned, then made a popping sound, pulling the head of Khafre's dick out of her mouth.

"I fucking love you too, nigga!"

Ketta deep-throated Khafre's dick a few more times, then mounted him cowgirl style. Khafre gripped her hair like a pair of reins, snapping her head back.

"Ffuuck yea!" Ketta said, bouncing up and down while grabbing her titties and pinching her nipples.

"Skeet on that dick!" Khafre demanded, letting her hair go.

"Yes, daddy!" Ketta leaned forward, placed her hands on Khafre's knees and rode him wild and hard.

146

Smack!

"What the fuck I told you?" *Smack!* Khafre slapped Ketta on her ass aggressively with the precise amount of pressure, driving her to an insane state of bliss.

"Sss—Ooowhooo, daddy, pussy skeetin on that dick! Aaaahh—Shit!"

Smack!

Khafre delivered another slap, causing Ketta to shake ungovernably. *Smack!*

"Ssss—Whoo! Stop! Don't—Sss—Don't—Sss—don't touch—me!" Ketta continued to shake for a full two minutes before gaining control of herself.

"Shit, daddy," Ketta moaned, climbing off Khafre's dick and cleaning it with her mouth. When she finished, she climbed up Khafre's body, placed her chin on his chest, and gazed at him ambivalently.

"I missed you, baby. I thought I'd never see you again!" Ketta remarked.

"I miss you more," Khafre replied.

"How'd you get in here?"

"Back door was open."

"Lies."

Khafre chuckled dryly.

"Wassup with Assata?"

"She good. I hope she didn't hear us," exclaimed Ketta.

Khafre's mind drifted off into suspended animation.

"Bae!" Ketta called to bring him back to reality.

"Wassup?" he replied.

Ketta laid her head on his chest and rubbed it up and down tenderly.

"How could you put yourself in a position to be taken away from me, away from your family?" Ketta's voice cracked as tears spilled from her eyes.

"Blood already spilt. I'm off that, ya hear me? Just make sho' my daughter straight!" he retorted laconically.

"And Hassan?"

"If he wakes up, he'll know what to do."

"You heard about your mother?"

Khafre inhaled then exhaled deeply.

"Yea."

"Them charges against her crazy," added Ketta.

Khafre kissed Ketta, then climbed out the bed.

"I'm finna go check on my daughter," Khafre stated, not wanting to talk about his situation.

"Okay," Ketta replied just above a whisper.

When Khafre left the room, Ketta allowed tears to flow freely down her face onto the pillow.

Khafre found Assata sleeping soundly. He approached the bed, bent down and placed a kiss on her forehead.

"I love you, baby girl."

Chapter Thirty-Five
Billy Bad Azz

"Miss Ketta, Miss Ketta, you up?" Assata called out on her way to Ketta's room. Ketta stirred, stretched, then yawned. When she opened her eyes, she found Assata standing in front of her bed. Looking on the other side of her bed, Ketta was disappointed to find Khafre gone.

"Yea, I'm up. Somebody in there?" Ketta questioned.

"Somebody like who? You expecting somebody?" Assata replied.

Assata couldn't have known her father was here, Ketta thought to herself.

Not wanting Assata to feel bad about Khafre not waking her up, Ketta decided to keep Khafre's visit to herself.

"No, I'm not expecting nobody. Wassup witchu though? You a'ight, you hungry?"

"I really don't have an appetite, but I did wanna go check on grandma," Assata said, looking and sounding emotionally fatigued.

"Okay. I had that on my agenda for today anyway. Before we leave, put something in your stomach!" Ketta suggested, climbing out of the bed, heading towards the shower.

"Fine," Assata said dryly.

***

Ketta placed her service weapon in between her seat and the console before pulling in her driveway.

"What kind of caliber is that?" Assata asked.

".40 caliber, why?" Ketta said, raising her eyebrows.

"Just asking."

"You sho?"

Assata nodded.

"What school you go to?"

"My daddy made all us do home schooling."

"That's gotta be boring. You don't have any friends?" Ketta questioned, pulling up to the red light on 25th and Avenue Q.

"No," Assata replied, letting her window down.

"Assata, I got the AC on. Why you rolled the window down?"

Assata snatched Ketta's service weapon, aimed it at the car to the right of them and squeezed.

"Assata!"

Assata squeezed again, but nothing happened. The car ran the red light, almost causing a collision. Ketta snatched the gun from Assata and made a left on Avenue Q.

"What the hell was that?" Ketta asked, her heart rate increasing.

Assata sat back in her seat calmly.

"I saw one of the guys who shot my brother," she stated with an air of dismissal.

"Well, damn! You could have said something. It's better ways to handle them type of situations." Ketta glanced at Assata, still shocked.

"I didn't know you were wit' the shits. You the police?"

"Yo' father ain't tell you 'bout me?"

"Only that he loves you."

"He told you that?"

Assata nodded.

"You gone see what I'm on. I gotchu, okay?"

"I hear you. What's wrong witcha gun?"

"It was on safety, Billy Bad Azz."

Ketta and Assata both laughed as Ketta pulled in front of Shantel's house.

"You think grandma going to do a lot of time?"

"I don't know," Ketta admitted, stepping out of her Benz truck.

Assata stepped out behind her and followed Ketta to the front door. Ketta knocked on the door and waited a moment.

"Shantel! It's Ketta!"

Assata turned the knob and the door opened.

"It's open, Assata stated. "She prolly in here sleep." The duo entered the home.

"Grandma!" Assata yelled then flopped down on the sofa.

Ketta headed to Shantel's room.

"Shantel, girl you got to come—Oh my gawd!" Ketta yelled in a tone that implied something was wrong.

"What!" Assata screamed before running into the room.

When Assata made it to the room, she found Shantel slumped over in her bed with her head blown off, and a suicide note on the nightstand. Assata fell to her knees.

"Grandma, noooooo!" Assata wailed relentlessly.

Tears fell from Ketta's eyes as she grabbed the note and read it.

Assata,
I know most likely you'll be the one to discover my body. You're the only one who stops by to check on me. Well, you and Hassan. Speaking of Hassan, when he wakes up, let him know that I love him so much. Y'all take care of each other, because y'all the last ones left in our bloodline. As much as I would love to stick around, I had to go. I cannot go to prison! I'm too old, and the feds took everything I had. They also wanted me to tell on my son, and that would never happen! I'd rather die! I know you're probably crying but wipe away those tears. I'm at peace. I love you with all my heart!
Love,

Grandma
P.S. Ketta's a good woman. Learn to love her, as she will you.

After the reading of the letter, Ketta tucked it and reached for Assata.

"Come on baby, we gotta go."

Chapter Thirty-Six

Never Return

It was a quarter after nine p.m. when Khafre slithered behind the brown store and knocked on the back door to Wolly's store. Wolly opened the slot and saw that it was Khafre. He opened the door.

"Khafre," Wolly spoke in his strong Arabic accent.

"Wassup, Wolly?" Khafre said, stepping inside the store.

"Give me a minute," Wolly said, then headed to the front of the store to lock it. "Come," Wolly motioned for Khafre to follow him to his safe room. Once the door was secure, Wolly spoke.

"Khafre, what the fuck!" Wolly snapped, throwing his hands in the air.

Khafre exhaled, seething.

"Some nigga I dealt wit' 'bout two years ago got me caught up in a conspiracy."

"And he's still alive?" Wolly questioned, frowning deeply.

"I been took care of it, but the investigation had already started. They don't need him. And on top of that, I was being followed. I thought somebody put a ticket on my head, so I ended up killing two federal agents, thinking it was a hit."

"Remove your shirt," demanded Wolly, pulling his pistol swiftly from his waist.

"You serious?"

"Quickly!"

Khafre shook his head in disbelief, then removed his shirt.

"You like a father to me! I'll never fuck you over!"

"Just had to make sure. Relax, buddy."

"Whatever, man. You tried my gangsta," exclaimed Khafre, putting his shirt back on.

"Listen to me, Khafre, you have to leave the country, and never return. Your presence is a threat to both of our freedom."

"Leave where?"

"I can get you into Africa safely, but you have to remain there forever! You'll be in a small village, but you'll be treated like a king, my friend."

"I can't go to Africa right na. I'ma just keep slippin' in and out. I gotta be close to my daughter and son."

Wolly shook his head in disgust. "I knew you would say that. Fine."

Wolly grabbed a bottle of Dewar's whisky, took a shot and handed the bottle to Khafre.

"You have my money?"

"No, they took everything," Khafre said with irritation in his tone.

He then took a long swig from the bottle of liquor. Wolly opened his safe and gave Khafre ten thousand dollars.

"Thanks, ock."

"Yea, you have to go now, my friend. Don't ever come back here. You hear me?" Wolly said, like a threat.

"Yea, ock. I hear you," Khafre replied, grabbing the money and turning to walk away.

"Khafre!"

"Yea?"

"Sorry about your mother."

***

After leaving Wolly's store, Khafre managed to make it to Lexus's apartment without being noticed. It had been a while since he seen or heard from Lexus, but after sweet-talking her out of her panties, Khafre convinced her to let him hold her car. In front of her apartment, he sat in the driver's seat, finishing off the bottle of whisky and plotting his next move. He was in deep thought when a black van pulled on the side of him. Startled, he grabbed his Glock-22 and raised it, but quickly lowered it when he saw a beautiful Israeli woman and her child exit the van.

"Damn, she gorgeous," Khafre thought out loud. He took another swig, then enjoyed the switch in the mysterious woman hips. Captivated by her booty, he didn't even hear the door slide on the van next to him. Khafre's door was snatched open, and he was pulled out aggressively. When he looked up, he saw two masked men holding state-of-the art weapons. They cursed and spoke in foreign vernacular while forcing him into the van. Once in the van, Khafre wasn't surprised to see more masked men, but he was confounded to see that same Israeli woman in the driver's seat.

"This can't be no fucking feds," Khafre muttered.

Chapter Thirty-Seven

Pooh Daddy

One Year Later—

"Assata, run in there and get us some chicken and gizzards. Make sho' you add extra hot sauce, ketchup, and peppers. And tell Wolly to load that shit up," exclaimed Ketta, handing Assata a twenty-dollar bill.

"Okay," Assata replied, getting out of the car. When she entered the store, Wolly was taking care of a customer, but still acknowledged her.

"Assata, baby, how are you?" Wolly asked as he finished serving a customer.

"I'm good, how bout'cha self?" she replied, handing Wolly the twenty dollars.

"I'm fine, and I keep telling you your money no good here. Take what you want," proclaimed Wolly, pushing the money back towards Assata.

"Thank you, Wolly. Let me get some chicken and gizzards fully loaded."

"Coming right up."

Assata took her phone out and checked her Facebook page. She saw that Lee Lee had posted a picture of them and hearted the picture.

"Damn, lil' moma, wassup?"

Assata turned around and saw a face she didn't recognize. She could tell whoever he was appeared to be hyped up on Molly. His lips were chapped, and he couldn't stop moving. Assata turned her back on him and ignored him.

"Damn, it's like that? My name Pooh Daddy! You heard of me?" Pooh Daddy asked.

"I'm from Duce Trey!" he stated, proudly licking his lips.

"Gone 'head on, man," Assata retorted, still surfing Facebook.

"Shid...bust it for me!" said Pooh Daddy, grabbing Assata's ass.

"Pussy nigga! Don't put yo dirty ass hands on me! Stupid ass fuck nigga!"

"What, hoe?" *Smack!* Pooh Daddy slapped Assata, causing her to knock over the chip rack and hit the floor.

"Okay, buddy! Leave my store now!" Wolly warned.

Pooh Daddy stood over Assata.

"Who the fuck you think you talking to, hoe? This Pooh Daddy, Bitch!"

"Last warning, buddy!" Wolly stated.

"Damn, Wolly. You gone check me 'bout a bitch? All the money I spend in this motherfucka!" Pooh Daddy yelled.

Boc!

Pooh Daddy's brains rained all over the countertop and can sodas before dropping to the floor hard.

"Pussy ass nigga!" Assata spat, standing to her feet with a micro compact .40 caliber.

Ketta had given it to her for her 15th birthday. Assata stood over Pooh Daddy, ready for overkill, but Wolly stopped her.

"Assata, he's already dead. Give me the gun and go. I'll take care of it." Wolly attempted to grab the pistol, when the door to the store swung open.

"Police! Freeze! Drop the weapon! Now!"

As soon as Assata saw the police, she thought of her father and everything she been through.

"Last warning! Drop—the—fucking—weapon! Now!"

To be continued...

156

Coming soon:
**Killa Kounty 5
(The Bloody Godmother)**

Lock Down Publications and Ca$h Presents
Assisted Publishing Packages

BASIC PACKAGE	UPGRADED PACKAGE
$499	$800
Editing	Typing
Cover Design	Editing
Formatting	Cover Design
	Formatting
ADVANCE PACKAGE	**LDP SUPREME PACKAGE**
$1,200	$1,500
Typing	Typing
Editing	Editing
Cover Design	Cover Design
Formatting	Formatting
Copyright registration	Copyright registration
Proofreading	Proofreading
Upload book to Amazon	Set up Amazon account
	Upload book to Amazon
	Advertise on LDP, Amazon and Facebook Page

***Other services available upon request.
Additional charges may apply
Lock Down Publications
P.O. Box 944
Stockbridge, GA 30281-9998
Phone: 470 303-9761

Submission Guideline

Submit the first three chapters of your completed manuscript to ldpsubmissions@gmail.com, subject line:

Your book's title. The manuscript must be in a .doc file and sent as an attachment. Document should be in Times New Roman, double spaced and in size 12 font. Also, provide your synopsis and full contact information. If sending multiple submissions, they must each be in a separate email.

Have a story but no way to send it electronically? You can still submit to LDP/Ca$h Presents. Send in the first three chapters, written or typed, of your completed manuscript to:

LDP: Submissions Dept
Po Box 944
Stockbridge, Ga 30281

DO NOT send original manuscript. Must be a duplicate.

Provide your synopsis and a cover letter containing your full contact information.

Thanks for considering LDP and Ca$h Presents.

NEW RELEASES

SOSA GANG 2 by ROMELL TUKES
KINGZ OF THE GAME 7 by PLAYA RAY
SKI MASK MONEY 2 by RENTA
BORN IN THE GRAVE 3 by SELF MADE TAY
LOYALTY IS EVERYTHING 3 by MOLOTTI

Coming Soon from Lock Down Publications/Ca$h Presents

BLOOD OF A BOSS **VI**

SHADOWS OF THE GAME II

TRAP BASTARD II

By Askari

LOYAL TO THE GAME **IV**

By T.J. & Jelissa

TRUE SAVAGE **VIII**

MIDNIGHT CARTEL IV

DOPE BOY MAGIC IV

CITY OF KINGZ III

NIGHTMARE ON SILENT AVE II

THE PLUG OF LIL MEXICO II

CLASSIC CITY II

By Chris Green

BLAST FOR ME **III**

A SAVAGE DOPEBOY III

CUTTHROAT MAFIA III

DUFFLE BAG CARTEL VII

HEARTLESS GOON VI

By Ghost

A HUSTLER'S DECEIT III

KILL ZONE II

BAE BELONGS TO ME III

TIL DEATH II

By Aryanna

KING OF THE TRAP III

By T.J. Edwards

GORILLAZ IN THE BAY V

3X KRAZY III

STRAIGHT BEAST MODE III

De'Kari

KINGPIN KILLAZ IV

STREET KINGS III
PAID IN BLOOD III
CARTEL KILLAZ IV
DOPE GODS III
Hood Rich
SINS OF A HUSTLA II
ASAD
YAYO V
Bred In The Game 2
S. Allen
THE STREETS WILL TALK II
By Yolanda Moore
SON OF A DOPE FIEND III
HEAVEN GOT A GHETTO III
SKI MASK MONEY III
By Renta
LOYALTY AIN'T PROMISED III
By Keith Williams
I'M NOTHING WITHOUT HIS LOVE II
SINS OF A THUG II
TO THE THUG I LOVED BEFORE II
IN A HUSTLER I TRUST II
By Monet Dragun
QUIET MONEY IV
EXTENDED CLIP III
THUG LIFE IV
By Trai'Quan
THE STREETS MADE ME IV
By Larry D. Wright
IF YOU CROSS ME ONCE III
ANGEL V
By Anthony Fields
THE STREETS WILL NEVER CLOSE IV
By K'ajji

HARD AND RUTHLESS III
KILLA KOUNTY IV
By Khufu
MONEY GAME III
By Smoove Dolla
JACK BOYS VS DOPE BOYS IV
A GANGSTA'S QUR'AN V
COKE GIRLZ II
COKE BOYS II
LIFE OF A SAVAGE V
CHI'RAQ GANGSTAS V
SOSA GANG III
BRONX SAVAGES II
BODYMORE KINGPINS II
By Romell Tukes
MURDA WAS THE CASE III
Elijah R. Freeman
AN UNFORESEEN LOVE IV
BABY, I'M WINTERTIME COLD III
By Meesha

QUEEN OF THE ZOO III
By Black Migo
CONFESSIONS OF A JACKBOY III
By Nicholas Lock
KING KILLA II
By Vincent "Vitto" Holloway
BETRAYAL OF A THUG III
By Fre$h
THE MURDER QUEENS III
By Michael Gallon
THE BIRTH OF A GANGSTER III
By Delmont Player
TREAL LOVE II
By Le'Monica Jackson
FOR THE LOVE OF BLOOD III

Available Now

RESTRAINING ORDER **I & II**
By CA$H & Coffee
LOVE KNOWS NO BOUNDARIES **I II & III**
By Coffee
RAISED AS A GOON I, II, III & IV
BRED BY THE SLUMS I, II, III
BLAST FOR ME I & II
ROTTEN TO THE CORE I II III
A BRONX TALE I, II, III
DUFFLE BAG CARTEL I II III IV V VI
HEARTLESS GOON I II III IV V
A SAVAGE DOPEBOY I II
DRUG LORDS I II III
CUTTHROAT MAFIA I II
KING OF THE TRENCHES
By Ghost
LAY IT DOWN **I & II**
LAST OF A DYING BREED I II
BLOOD STAINS OF A SHOTTA I & II III
By Jamaica
LOYAL TO THE GAME I II III
LIFE OF SIN I, II III
By TJ & Jelissa
BLOODY COMMAS I & II
SKI MASK CARTEL I II & III
KING OF NEW YORK I II,III IV V
RISE TO POWER I II III
COKE KINGS I II III IV V
BORN HEARTLESS I II III IV
KING OF THE TRAP I II
By T.J. Edwards
IF LOVING HIM IS WRONG…I & II
LOVE ME EVEN WHEN IT HURTS I II III
By Jelissa

WHEN THE STREETS CLAP BACK I & II III
THE HEART OF A SAVAGE I II III IV
MONEY MAFIA I II
LOYAL TO THE SOIL I II III
By Jibril Williams
A DISTINGUISHED THUG STOLE MY HEART I II & III
LOVE SHOULDN'T HURT I II III IV
RENEGADE BOYS I II III IV
PAID IN KARMA I II III
SAVAGE STORMS I II III
AN UNFORESEEN LOVE I II III
BABY, I'M WINTERTIME COLD I II
By Meesha
A GANGSTER'S CODE I &, II III
A GANGSTER'S SYN I II III
THE SAVAGE LIFE I II III
CHAINED TO THE STREETS I II III
BLOOD ON THE MONEY I II III
A GANGSTA'S PAIN I II III
By J-Blunt
PUSH IT TO THE LIMIT
By Bre' Hayes
BLOOD OF A BOSS I, II, III, IV, V
SHADOWS OF THE GAME
TRAP BASTARD
By Askari
THE STREETS BLEED MURDER **I, II & III**
THE HEART OF A GANGSTA I II& III
By Jerry Jackson
CUM FOR ME I II III IV V VI VII VIII
An LDP Erotica Collaboration
BRIDE OF A HUSTLA **I II & II**
THE FETTI GIRLS **I, II& III**

CORRUPTED BY A GANGSTA I, II III, IV
BLINDED BY HIS LOVE
THE PRICE YOU PAY FOR LOVE I, II ,III
DOPE GIRL MAGIC I II III
By Destiny Skai
WHEN A GOOD GIRL GOES BAD
By Adrienne
THE COST OF LOYALTY I II III
By Kweli
A GANGSTER'S REVENGE **I II III & IV**
THE BOSS MAN'S DAUGHTERS I II III IV V
A SAVAGE LOVE **I & II**
BAE BELONGS TO ME I II
A HUSTLER'S DECEIT I, II, III
WHAT BAD BITCHES DO I, II, III
SOUL OF A MONSTER I II III
KILL ZONE
A DOPE BOY'S QUEEN I II III
TIL DEATH
By Aryanna
A KINGPIN'S AMBITON
A KINGPIN'S AMBITION **II**
I MURDER FOR THE DOUGH
By Ambitious
TRUE SAVAGE I II III IV V VI VII
DOPE BOY MAGIC I, II, III
MIDNIGHT CARTEL I II III
CITY OF KINGZ I II
NIGHTMARE ON SILENT AVE
THE PLUG OF LIL MEXICO II
CLASSIC CITY
By Chris Green
A DOPEBOY'S PRAYER
By Eddie "Wolf" Lee
THE KING CARTEL **I, II & III**
By Frank Gresham

THESE NIGGAS AIN'T LOYAL **I, II & III**
By Nikki Tee
GANGSTA SHYT **I II &III**
By CATO
THE ULTIMATE BETRAYAL
By Phoenix
Boss'n Up i , ii & IIi
By Royal Nicole
I LOVE YOU TO DEATH
By Destiny J
I RIDE FOR MY HITTA
I STILL RIDE FOR MY HITTA
By Misty Holt
LOVE & CHASIN' PAPER
By Qay Crockett
TO DIE IN VAIN
SINS OF A HUSTLA
By ASAD
BROOKLYN HUSTLAZ
By Boogsy Morina
BROOKLYN ON LOCK I & II
By Sonovia
GANGSTA CITY
By Teddy Duke
A DRUG KING AND HIS DIAMOND I & II III
A DOPEMAN'S RICHES
HER MAN, MINE'S TOO I, II
CASH MONEY HO'S
THE WIFEY I USED TO BE I II
PRETTY GIRLS DO NASTY THINGS
By Nicole Goosby
TRAPHOUSE KING **I II & III**
KINGPIN KILLAZ I II III
STREET KINGS I II

168

PAID IN BLOOD **I II**
CARTEL KILLAZ I II III
DOPE GODS I II
By Hood Rich
LIPSTICK KILLAH **I, II, III**
CRIME OF PASSION I II & III
FRIEND OR FOE I II III
By Mimi
STEADY MOBBN' **I, II, III**
THE STREETS STAINED MY SOUL I II III
By Marcellus Allen
WHO SHOT YA **I, II, III**
SON OF A DOPE FIEND I II
HEAVEN GOT A GHETTO I II
SKI MASK MONEY I II
Renta
GORILLAZ IN THE BAY **I II III IV**
TEARS OF A GANGSTA I II
3X KRAZY I II
STRAIGHT BEAST MODE I II
DE'KARI
TRIGGADALE I II III
MURDAROBER WAS THE CASE I II
Elijah R. Freeman
GOD BLESS THE TRAPPERS I, II, III
THESE SCANDALOUS STREETS I, II, III
FEAR MY GANGSTA I, II, III IV, V
THESE STREETS DON'T LOVE NOBODY I, II
BURY ME A G I, II, III, IV, V
A GANGSTA'S EMPIRE I, II, III, IV
THE DOPEMAN'S BODYGAURD I II
THE REALEST KILLAZ I II III
THE LAST OF THE OGS I II III
Tranay Adams
THE STREETS ARE CALLING
Duquie Wilson

MARRIED TO A BOSS I II III
By Destiny Skai & Chris Green
KINGZ OF THE GAME I II III IV V VI VII
CRIME BOSS
Playa Ray
SLAUGHTER GANG I II III
RUTHLESS HEART I II III
By Willie Slaughter
FUK SHYT
By Blakk Diamond
DON'T F#CK WITH MY HEART I II
By Linnea
ADDICTED TO THE DRAMA I II III
IN THE ARM OF HIS BOSS II
By Jamila
YAYO I II III IV
A SHOOTER'S AMBITION I II
BRED IN THE GAME
By S. Allen
TRAP GOD I II III
RICH $AVAGE I II III
MONEY IN THE GRAVE I II III
By Martell Troublesome Bolden
FOREVER GANGSTA I II
 GLOCKS ON SATIN SHEETS I II
By Adrian Dulan
TOE TAGZ I II III IV
LEVELS TO THIS SHYT I II
IT'S JUST ME AND YOU
By Ah'Million
KINGPIN DREAMS I II III
RAN OFF ON DA PLUG
By Paper Boi Rari
CONFESSIONS OF A GANGSTA I II III IV

CONFESSIONS OF A JACKBOY I II
By Nicholas Lock
I'M NOTHING WITHOUT HIS LOVE
SINS OF A THUG
TO THE THUG I LOVED BEFORE
A GANGSTA SAVED XMAS
IN A HUSTLER I TRUST
By Monet Dragun
CAUGHT UP IN THE LIFE I II III
THE STREETS NEVER LET GO I II III
By Robert Baptiste
NEW TO THE GAME I II III
MONEY, MURDER & MEMORIES I II III
By Malik D. Rice
LIFE OF A SAVAGE I II III IV
A GANGSTA'S QUR'AN I II III IV
MURDA SEASON I II III
GANGLAND CARTEL I II III
CHI'RAQ GANGSTAS I II III IV
KILLERS ON ELM STREET I II III
JACK BOYZ N DA BRONX I II III
A DOPEBOY'S DREAM I II III
JACK BOYS VS DOPE BOYS I II III
COKE GIRLZ
COKE BOYS
SOSA GANG I II
BRONX SAVAGES
BODYMORE KINGPINS
By Romell Tukes
LOYALTY AIN'T PROMISED I II
By Keith Williams
QUIET MONEY I II III
THUG LIFE I II III
EXTENDED CLIP I II
A GANGSTA'S PARADISE
By Trai'Quan

THE STREETS MADE ME I II III
By Larry D. Wright
THE ULTIMATE SACRIFICE I, II, III, IV, V, VI
KHADIFI
IF YOU CROSS ME ONCE I II
ANGEL I II III IV
IN THE BLINK OF AN EYE
By Anthony Fields
THE LIFE OF A HOOD STAR
By Ca$h & Rashia Wilson
THE STREETS WILL NEVER CLOSE I II III
By K'ajji
CREAM I II III
THE STREETS WILL TALK
By Yolanda Moore
NIGHTMARES OF A HUSTLA I II III
By King Dream
CONCRETE KILLA I II III
VICIOUS LOYALTY I II III
By Kingpen
HARD AND RUTHLESS I II
MOB TOWN 251
THE BILLIONAIRE BENTLEYS I II III
REAL G'S MOVE IN SILENCE
By Von Diesel
GHOST MOB
Stilloan Robinson
MOB TIES I II III IV V VI
SOUL OF A HUSTLER, HEART OF A KILLER I II
GORILLAZ IN THE TRENCHES
By SayNoMore
BODYMORE MURDERLAND I II III
THE BIRTH OF A GANGSTER I II
By Delmont Player

FOR THE LOVE OF A BOSS
By C. D. Blue
MOBBED UP I II III IV
THE BRICK MAN I II III IV V
THE COCAINE PRINCESS I II III IV V VI VII
By King Rio
KILLA KOUNTY I II III IV
By Khufu
MONEY GAME I II
By Smoove Dolla
A GANGSTA'S KARMA I II III
By FLAME
KING OF THE TRENCHES I II III
by GHOST & TRANAY ADAMS
QUEEN OF THE ZOO I II
By Black Migo
GRIMEY WAYS I II III
By Ray Vinci
XMAS WITH AN ATL SHOOTER
By Ca$h & Destiny Skai
KING KILLA
By Vincent "Vitto" Holloway
BETRAYAL OF A THUG I II
By Fre$h
THE MURDER QUEENS I II
By Michael Gallon
TREAL LOVE
By Le'Monica Jackson
FOR THE LOVE OF BLOOD I II
By Jamel Mitchell
HOOD CONSIGLIERE I II
By Keese
PROTÉGÉ OF A LEGEND I II
LOVE IN THE TRENCHES
By Corey Robinson
BORN IN THE GRAVE I II III

By Self Made Tay
MOAN IN MY MOUTH
By XTASY
TORN BETWEEN A GANGSTER AND A
GENTLEMAN
By J-BLUNT & Miss Kim
LOYALTY IS EVERYTHING I II
Molotti
HERE TODAY GONE TOMORROW
By Fly Rock
PILLOW PRINCESS
By S. Hawkins

BOOKS BY LDP'S CEO, CA$H

TRUST IN NO MAN
TRUST IN NO MAN 2
TRUST IN NO MAN 3
BONDED BY BLOOD
SHORTY GOT A THUG
THUGS CRY
THUGS CRY 2
THUGS CRY 3
TRUST NO BITCH
TRUST NO BITCH 2
TRUST NO BITCH 3
TIL MY CASKET DROPS
RESTRAINING ORDER
RESTRAINING ORDER 2
IN LOVE WITH A CONVICT
LIFE OF A HOOD STAR
XMAS WITH AN ATL SHOOTER